PHOTO CHUTE

ROCKIN' RODEO SERIES 2

VICKI THARP

JPC PUBLISHING

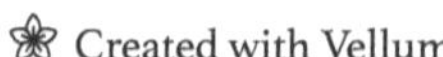 Created with Vellum

PHOTO CHUTE

1

———

IAN MURPHY STOOD RIGID IN FRONT OF THE TATTERED OAK DESK, the one with the stack of old phone books propping up one corner, waiting for his father to stop laughing at him.

The scent of sweat, grease and old gas sat heavy in his father's office of Murphy's Auto Repair, but not as heavy as the must and mold. Ian dug his grease-stained hands deep into the pockets of his work coveralls. "I don't see what's so bleeding funny."

His father swiped the moisture away from his eyes and took a deep breath but couldn't hold back one more disparaging chuckle. "You. A cowboy."

Patrick Murphy spat the word 'cowboy', the way the old biddies at church said the word 'whore'—a job prospect he might have to revisit if Ian didn't get that overseas assignment he had his eye on. One more oppressive day at the shop wasn't an option.

"Do ye even know which end of the bull has the horns?"

"I'm not trying to be a cowboy, Da. I'm just going to follow the winter rodeo circuit and photograph them."

"Why the bloody hell would ye want to do that?" His father's

Irish brogue was still thick even though his parents had immigrated to New York way before Ian had been brought into the world.

"To prove to *GlobeTrotter Magazine* that I can fit in where I don't belong. That I can become a fly on the stall, so to speak, and get the behind-the-scenes shots the magazine is known for. The people. Their hearts. Their stories. Their *humanity*."

The smile slipped from his father's face, replaced by that look of derision that usually marred his face whenever he looked at Ian. "For fucks sake, lad, what makes ye think ye can fit in there when ye can't even fit in here?"

Can't argue the truth. All Ian knew was that if he won this contest, he could possibly win one of the magazine's few coveted international slots.

A heart murmur had kept him from shipping out to Vietnam, but maybe he could serve his country with his camera. *His* photographs, *his* stories, splashed across the center of a magazine seen by millions of people every month.

If everyone knew his name, he couldn't be an outcast.

"I'm a grown man. I'm—"

"Yer nothin' but a pup—"

"I'm twenty-four, Da, and I'm not asking for permission, or even your blessing. All I want to know is if you'll sell me the old camper. It hasn't been used since—" Ian cut himself off before his throat got too tight to speak. It had been almost fifteen years since his mother's death, and he still got choked up.

Unlike his father and older brothers who seemed to have moved on with their lives as if they'd lost their wallet, not their mother or their wife.

"It hasn't been used in a long time," Ian said. "It's sitting in the repair yard taking up space."

The office door opened and Sean, one of Ian's older brothers, stuck his head in. Sean's neck was thick like the rest of him. His ginger hair cut short above his ears.

If his family were suitcases, and you stacked his grandfather, his father, and his two brothers' side by side, they would be a matched set. Hefty. Rugged. Well made.

Then there was Ian.

A scruffier, lighter weight piece thrown in as an afterthought to carry the dirty shoes.

"Get ye arse back in the bay," Sean said. "That carburetor won't change itself, no?"

"Yeah, yeah," Ian said, "Keep your knickers on."

Sean flipped him off but closed the door. Ian pulled his wallet out of his pocket and peeled off four, one-hundred-dollar bills from his dwindling stack of cash. "I called around. Four hundred is more than a fair price for that camper."

He tossed the bills on top of the grease smudged file folders and repair receipts. Patrick Murphy rarely turned down a fistful of cash.

His father eyed him but picked up the money and slipped it into the breast pocket of his work shirt, studying him as he buttoned the flap. "You want out of this family that bad?"

"It's hard to be out of something you never felt like you were in." There. He'd said it. Ian waited for his father's denial.

It didn't come.

"Your mother spoiled you."

Spoiled him?

Heat spit and sparked in Ian's veins until his heart kicked at his ribs and the blood vessel at his temple ticked. "You call it spoiling when Ma protected me from a father who was quick with his temper and even quicker with a belt? You call it spoiling when Ma pulled me from the bottom of a human dogpile when my brothers—my much older, much bigger brothers—thought it was fun to use me as their personal punching bag?"

If that was the case, then yeah, he was *spoiled*.

"Twas for ye own good, it was. Ye learned how ta fight like a proper lad. Blokes don't push ye around. No matter what happened, *my* responsibility ye were. You'd rather I let ye grow up to be a right pussy like yer—"

Ian's father cut himself off, his mouth screwing up, his face turning red, as if the unsaid words on his tongue tasted like shite.

Leaning across the desk, Ian slapped a hand on the wood so hard it reverberated up his arm and into his shoulder. "Like my *what*?"

His father stood, his hands on the desk like Ian's own, his face inches away. Ian smelled the salami on his father's breath from the deli down the street. "Like your real da."

His real *father*.

The truth.

Ian's breath rushed out in an audible whoosh, the center of his chest stung, and he couldn't breathe like all those times when his brothers would take him to the ground with a sucker punch to the solar plexus.

Sweat pricked along Ian's hairline and his knees went to liquid. He needed to sit before he fell, but he couldn't let his Da see that he'd landed a stunning blow. Ian straightened, widening his stance, and locking his knees.

At least that explained why the man in front of him had always treated Ian like a pariah. Or worse.

It also explained why Ian had never felt like he fit in. Why he wasn't built like his father and brothers. Why his hair was dark while his father and brothers were fair.

His mother had cheated.

Even as the thought came to his head, he couldn't be mad at his mother. She'd deserved so much better than his father...make that his step-father. "How do you know I'm not yours?"

"Your mother always wanted a big family, but two screaming babies was enough for me. I had me-self snipped, me did. She thought the problem was her." His father shrugged. "She said ye were a right miracle, you was."

"You didn't tell her you had a vasectomy?"

"Had the big blue balls ta prove it."

Ian scrunched up his face but couldn't erase the disturbing mental image. "Who was he?"

"Never asked."

"But all those years, you let Ma believe you thought I was yours."

His father sat, and only shrugged one shoulder as if he couldn't be arsed to shrug with two. "Acht, she knew, but neither of us let on. I raised ye as my own."

"No." Ian couldn't keep the bitterness from creeping into his voice. "You may have raised me, but I wasn't treated like one of your own."

His father looked back at him, more bored than upset by the accusation.

"When I was twelve and you caught me looking for my birth certificate because I thought I had been adopted, why didn't you tell me then?" Why hadn't he been told he was another man's bastard?

Ian didn't wait for an answer. He couldn't breathe. Couldn't get away from his father, from the garage, from the Bronx, from a life that was never really his, fast enough.

He strode to the door. It didn't matter that he hadn't been told. The past was the past. Halfway through the door, he turned back to his father—no, not his father. Ian didn't even know what to call him now, but he turned back and asked, "If you never knew my real father, how do you know he was a pussy?"

Patrick Murphy met Ian's eyes. One corner of his mouth curved into a sneer. "He never claimed ye, did he, lad?"

———

TWO BARRELS.

Cora Hayes hadn't dropped two barrels in a single barrel race since she was ten years old. Now she'd done it twice in a row. She'd lost her groove, and she'd lose the winter circuit buckle if she didn't find a way to get her groove back.

"You okay?" Josephine Cox asked, as she sat down beside Cora in the grass on the outskirts of the rodeo parking lot in El Paso, Texas.

The wind blew fast and hard in that part of Texas where there was nothing around them higher than the curb to block the biting wind. But Cora didn't even bother to button up her jacket all the way. She'd already lost feeling in the fingers she'd folded around Panache's lead rope. Her quarter horse gelding, and partner in crime, chomped away at the skinny strands of winter rye fighting through the red Texas clay.

Cora hadn't been this far from okay since she'd missed her period a couple months ago. "Not really."

Josephine was the only friend Cora trusted enough tell the truth. If anyone else would have asked, she would have screwed on a sickeningly-sweet smile, all teeth and feigned confidence, and said 'never better'.

But this was Josephine. Travel partner, bunk mate, best friend.

"It's early in the season," Josephine said. "Don't let it get to you. We all have bad runs."

"Not like this." Cora gave Panache's lead rope a light tug, so he wouldn't be pulling on her arm. He moved a couple steps closer and chomped away at the sweet grass, his blanket buckled tight around his belly, his eyelids heavy as he grazed, half asleep. "I've got a call in to the vet to come out and make sure Panache isn't sore in his shoulders, or if he has a lameness I can't see. Maybe that new saddle isn't fitting right."

Cora had her knees curled up to her chest for warmth. Josephine snaked her arm through Cora's. "Honey, save yourself some money. It isn't the horse, or the saddle. It's you."

Crap. She was afraid of that. Cora closed her eyes. Was it that obvious? "I don't know what else to do. I've tried giving him his head. I tried collecting him more. I tried lifting his shoulder in the turn. I tried adding pressure with my inside leg as I go into the first barrel. Nothing is working, and that buck he threw at the second barrel? What the hell was that all about? Panache never bucks."

"You've got to get back to the basics. Back to what works for you."

"No way. We're not going back to trotting the pattern. Panache would buck me off for sure." As if he understood her, Panache shook his head and blew out a nose full of dirt.

"Ewh." Josephine wiped the horsey snot from the sleeve of her jacket onto her jeans. "That's not what I meant, either."

"Then what?" Cora's voice rose, unable to squash the exasperation. At this rate she might as well cut her losses and get a job back home at the diner. At least then she'd be ahead in the money.

"Work with me here," Josephine said. "What were you doing last season when you were winning all the races that you aren't doing now?"

Josephine gave her a little nudge as if that would help Cora jog her memory.

Newsflash. It didn't. "For the love of God, woman. Please tell me."

"You need to get laid."

Cora laughed, letting the derision fly. "No thanks. Been there, done that, had the pregnancy scare to prove it."

"I get it. I do. But ever since you gave up men, your runs have looked more amateurish than the kiddie classes on 4–H night."

"Have not."

Josephine scoffed. "Have too."

The wind whipped up. Cora would turn into a human Popsicle if she stayed out much longer. She struggled to her feet and gave Josephine a hand up. With a soft cluck to Panache, the three of them headed back toward the barn. "What do you expect me to do? Go to the bar, pick up the first cowboy I see that strikes my fancy, and take him back to the trailer for the night?"

"Yes!" The ear-to-ear grin on Josephine's face reminded Cora of her old geometry teacher's when she'd answer a question right in front of the class. Cora remembered because it hadn't happened that often.

"Silas is driving in tonight," Josephine continued. "We're getting a motel." The way Josephine said 'motel', with her eyes all dreamy, you would have thought she'd said 'palace', and not meant the short strip of rooms with threadbare carpet and missing shingles on the roof. At least there was no rain in the forecast.

"I'm not bringing a guy to the trailer."

"Why not? You'll have it all to yourself." Josephine wasn't going to let it drop.

Their boots scuffed across the asphalt parking lot, the barn lights a beacon of warmth up ahead. They kept their arms linked, their bodies hunched together for warmth as they walked beside Panache and used his big muscular body as a walking windbreak.

"Having the trailer to myself isn't as much of an enticement as it used to be."

For most people on the circuit, motels were reserved for special occasions, like tonight, when the rodeo swung close enough for Josephine's fiancé, Silas Foss, to drive in for the weekend.

For the rest of the time, Josephine and Cora lived out of the front tack room of Josephine's bumper pull horse trailer that she'd outfitted as a mini camper. Emphasis on the 'mini'.

"Besides, because of 'the scare,'" Cora used finger quotes around the word 'scare,' "I wouldn't be able to get a guy to sleep with me even if I wanted to. You'd a thought I was going around poking holes in all my condoms. Trust me, I was way more freaked out than Levi."

"No one thinks that."

"Sure they don't."

At Panache's stall, Cora checked hay and water, and sent her horse into the stall. Panache gave Josephine's palomino a soft nicker in the adjoining stall, touching noses through the bars.

After removing the halter, her gelding dove nose first into his hay. Cora stepped out as one of the heelers Cora had dated a few times left his stall and walked toward them. The cowboy had always been very good with a rope both on ...and off...a horse. Plus, there was the whole thing about him never being able to turn down a good time. Here was Cora's chance to prove Josephine wrong.

Cora leaned in and whispered in Josephine's ear. "Watch this."

Caddo O'Shea was still three stalls away when Cora tucked a stray strand of hair behind her ear, turned up the wattage on her smile, and forced enthusiasm into her voice. "Hey, Caddo, you up for a beer tonight?"

Caddo drew up short. All six foot, two hundred and ten pounds of muscle and man. His eyes went wide as if he'd seen a Sasquatch lumbering down the aisle and not a pretty, petite, twenty-three-year-old barrel racer. "Um...hey." Then he tipped his hat toward Josephine. "Josie."

Josephine gave him a little wave. "Hey, Caddo."

Cora cocked a hip. "We're thinking of hitting The Wagon Wheel tonight. Wanna come?"

"Um... yeah...I gotta," Caddo glanced back at his horse as if his mare would help him out of a jamb. He hitched a finger over his shoulder towards his stall. "I gotta keep an eye on Flash, she's been off her feed."

Flash lifted her head, a huge hunk of alfalfa sticking out either side of her mouth, her eyes bright, her jaws crunching and munching away.

Cora's stomach took a dive. It wasn't that something was wrong with his horse, it was that something was wrong with her. She knew it, but it still hurt.

There came a loud whistle behind them, she turned to find Smokey Dunn, Caddo's team roping partner, standing at the end of the aisle. He made a 'come on' motion with his arm. "Get your ass moving, O'Shea, we're gonna miss our ride to The Wheel."

Caddo ducked his head, an apologetic tilt to his lying lips. "I-I better go. Good seeing you girls." After tipping his hat to them, he jogged down the aisle to catch up with his friend.

Cora slid her hand through the bars and plucked a piece of hay out of Panache's forelock. Before they left, Cora double checked the stall latch to make sure it was secure. "See? What did I tell you? I'm tainted. Like a beautiful flower everyone just discovered is poisonous."

"There are plenty more where he came from." Josephine tugged Cora's arm, walking backward, as she dragged her toward the parking lot. "Come with us. It's time to get you back in the saddle. What do you have to lose?"

Cora allowed herself to be hauled back to their trailer, the same way she was going to allow Josephine to haul her to The

Wheel. At this point, she was willing to try just about anything to get back to the top of the leader boards.

They passed a series of indoor chutes as some men from No Bull, one of a couple of roughstock suppliers who brought in all the bulls, the saddle broncs, and the roping steers for the rodeos, offloaded a truckload of calves. The animals bawled and moo'ed, as they pushed and shoved through the chutes, their hot breaths turning to vapor in the cold night air.

The nearest man stopped working and tipped his hat to them. He wasn't as big or as muscular as a lot of the cowboys, or nearly as good looking. One of the flag team girls described him as being two beers shy of being screw-able.

The girls weren't wrong, but since her pregnancy scare, Cora didn't care as much about those things. "Hey, Scottie," Cora said, "You're not letting them work you too hard, are you?"

He spit a shot of tobacco in the dirt at his feet. His teeth were stained, but the wattage meter on his smile hit sincere. "No, ma'am. We're about done for the night."

"I'm not even two years older than you. Drop the ma'am already."

Scottie palmed his cowboy hat and ran a hand through his hair. "Yes, ma'am."

One of the other men whistled at Scottie, and he turned back to finish the offloading. After leaving the barn, Cora glanced over at Josephine. She had this funny look on her face.

"What's wrong with you?" Cora asked. "You look amazed, like I walked on water or ran the barrel pattern buck naked. Which I would totally do on a bet if it weren't so freaking cold out. The barrel pattern, not the walking on water bit."

"Since when do you talk to Scottie Hines?"

"What's wrong with talking to Scottie?"

"You never seemed to notice him before, even though he'd noticed you. You never told me you two were friends." Cora couldn't read Josephine's expression, but the pinch of incredulity in her voice made Cora feel as if she'd come across as shallow and self-centered at times. Maybe she had. But she'd changed a lot since 'the scare.'

Cora shrugged. Best friends or not, for some reason she'd never told Josephine about her little melt down, and by 'little melt down' Cora meant the big boo-hoos, the snotty sniffles, the puffy-eyed, drink-half-the-bottle-of-booze kind of breakdown she'd had when she found out she wasn't pregnant. She hadn't known how freaked out she had been until she'd gotten her period three weeks late.

What a relief.

She wouldn't have had the words to tell her preacher father that his little girl had gone off to the circuit and gotten herself pregnant.

That's when Scottie had found her sitting in the back of the horse trailer. Crying with relief and celebrating with Jack...Daniels.

"We talked one night in Oklahoma City. I think that was when Silas came up and the two of you disappeared for a couple hours. That's when I'd found out—"

"Sorry about that, I hadn't seen him in—"

"No. It's fine. But since then, Scottie and I have been talking a bit. Or I guess I should say listening. He doesn't say much, but he's a great listener."

Josephine gave her a nudge with her elbow. "He seems kinda taken with you. Maybe you should invite—"

"It's not like that," Cora was quick to add. "We're friends. Or at least friendly. Nothing more."

They were in the darkest part of the parking lot between the barn and the area where all the rodeo people had parked their rigs. There were a few lights on here and there, but overhead, the stars were big and bright—a brilliant blanket of twinkling lights on a cold, clear Texas night. People were right when they said everything was bigger in Texas.

They made their way back to their trailer. Josephine had parked near one of the light poles in the middle of the parking lot, so they would have some light if they had to run to the porta-potty in the back of the trailer in the middle of the night.

"What's this?" Josephine said as she plucked a single red rose wedged in the door.

"Silas is sweet, but I didn't figure your fiancé for the kind of guy who showers his girl with flowers."

"He doesn't. Plus, he isn't here yet." Josephine plucked a card from the jamb and read the front of the envelope. "It's for you."

No one ever sent her flowers. Cora took the rose from Josephine's hand, pricked herself, and sucked the drop of blood from the end of her thumb. "Ouch." She tore the little card from the envelope and held it up to the light. "It says 'Better luck next time, beautiful.'"

Josephine got a devious glint in her eye. "'*Beautiful?*' Maybe this guy wants—"

Cora cut her a look. "Would you stop trying to get me laid?"

"Sorry." Josephine managed to sound a bit contrite, but her smile didn't make her look sorry at all. "Who's it from?"

Josephine rechecked the card and the envelope, but whoever had sent it hadn't left their name. "No clue."

"Oooh," Josephine said as she unlocked their door. "Someone has a secret admirer."

2

———

THE INSIDE OF THE WAGON WHEEL DIDN'T DISAPPOINT. IAN claimed a seat at the end of the bar, giving him a clear view of the rest of the joint. It had taken him three days, one flat tire, and one busted radiator to make it to El Paso, Texas. The last thing he should want to do is sit down, but exhaustion won out.

His wallet hadn't fared well, the trip and the repairs turned out to be more expensive than he'd anticipated. Not only had he left Murphy's Auto Repair in his rear-view window, he'd also cut off his main source of income.

Before he'd left New York, he'd packed his camper full of non-perishables, but now with his cash running short and free-lance photography as his only means of making money, if he didn't sell any photographs soon, he would starve.

A worry for another day. Tonight, he'd nurse a whiskey, have a hot meal at the bar, and spend a couple hours watching this group of people he'd have to infiltrate.

He'd need to find someone to befriend. Someone who could help him break into this tight knit community of cowboys. He recognized a few of the men from the parking lot of the rodeo arena where he'd dumped his camper for the night, but tonight was about observation, not implementation.

"Whiskey, and a menu," Ian told the bartender as he dropped his camera bag on the floor at his feet. "Make it a double."

Tall and lean, the bartender was probably the only one in the bar besides Ian who wasn't wearing a cowboy hat. The man dried the ring of moisture off the bar in front of Ian and gave him a suspicious look. "Where ya from?"

Even with Ian trying to flatten his New York accent, even over the bump and base of the country music pouring out of the speakers, those eight words had been all he'd had to say, and the bartender knew Ian didn't belong. Fitting in was going to be a lot harder than he'd thought. "Up north."

Ian didn't elaborate. The bartender didn't press.

While Ian waited for his drink, he pulled his camera out of his bag and set it on the bar. He loaded up a roll of black and white film, which he'd come to prefer over colored film. In a place like this bar with the low lights, he'd need the faster speed film if he hoped for any of the shots to come out without having to use a flash. Hard to go unnoticed if he was blinding everybody.

The bartender returned with his whiskey and after a quick glance at the menu, Ian ordered a chicken fried steak and mashed potatoes. He took a sip as his eyes skimmed around the inside of the bar. The live music came from a stage the size of a photo negative. The singer was some up and coming guy by the name of Hank Williams Jr. from what the fliers out front advertised.

Most of the tables were occupied, the voices a loud steady drone beneath the music. On the dance floor, couples danced slow and close. The front door opened, and a guy walked in with a brunette on his arm, but it was the brunette behind him that dazzled Ian.

Backlit from the stage lights, Ian's gaze traveled down her body from the sharp cut brim of her cowboy hat, to the fringe on the arms of her shirt, and down to the curve of her jeans-clad ass that made his heart kick and the crotch of his jeans get tight.

But it wasn't the sparkles on her shirt that dazzled him, it was the arresting way she confidently carried herself, her body language saying, here-I-am-world.

The sparkly woman walked toward one of the few empty tables and laughed at something the other woman said. Not a feminine little giggle. This was a head thrown back, all-out laugh that carried across the bar. He felt for his glass and brought it to his lips, unable to take his eyes off her.

She reached for a chair at one the empty tables as Ian reached for his camera, wanting to capture the perfection. He stopped himself.

As much as he wanted her on film, for once he didn't want that filter between him and real life, that extra lens that would tear him out of this world and drop him into another. A world where he sat on the sidelines and watched people live their lives through his camera's lens.

A world where he was on the outside looking in.

Someone dropped onto the stool beside him and ordered a beer. Ian didn't pay the man any mind, too busy drinking the woman in. Ian had come to take behind the scene photos of life on the rodeo circuit, but in his mind, he'd pictured dust and dung, sweaty men and determined faces. The battle between man and beast.

He hadn't expected *her*.

The man beside Ian said something. Ian refocused his gaze on his new drinking buddy. "What was that?"

The man was built like a tank with hard edges, massive biceps, and thick forearms. No, scratch that, not built like a tank, but he could probably bench press one.

The man pointed with his long-neck beer. "That's Cora Hayes. The woman you're staring at." The man had that look in his eye. Proprietary. Protective.

"I wasn't staring."

The man gave him the side eye. "Right."

Ian put his hands up, not knowing what this woman was to the stranger, but Ian was too road weary to fight. Besides, as good as Ian was in a brawl, the guy had to have fifty pounds on Ian. "I didn't mean nothin' by it."

"Didn't say you did." The man took a long drag of his beer, his eyes never leaving Ian's, then set the beer down and stuck out his hand. "Levi. Levi Banks."

Ian shook his hand. "Ian Murphy."

"You're not from around here." Not a question.

"Let me guess, the bloody accent gave me away." With the whiskey warming his veins, he let a little of the Irish brogue slip out. Normally he tried to hide it to fit in, but he was so far out of his element here, he might as well be himself.

Levi turned toward him and looked him up and down. "It wasn't the accent. It was the clothes."

"What's wrong with my clothes?"

"You look like a city slicker poser from up north trying to fit in."

The bartender dumped the chicken fried steak in front of Ian and he didn't waste a moment digging in. He cut off a slab and stuffed it into his mouth and watched Cora Hayes' table. The man and woman with her went off to dance leaving Cora alone at the table with a beer. She glanced at the front door the way a condemned man eyes the open jail cell.

Cora finished her beer and raised a hand to the waitress to bring her another.

"Again, what's wrong with that?"

Levi pushed up the brim of his hat. He didn't smile, but amusement lingered in his eyes. "Nothing, if you don't want a chance with Cora. She only dates cowboys."

Ian laughed and washed down a mouthful of mashed potatoes with a swallow of whiskey. He made a face. Mashed potatoes and whiskey, not a good combo. "I'm not here looking for sex."

"Then you'd be the only one."

Ian picked up his camera and gave it a waggle as if that explained everything. "I'm a freelance photographer."

"You following the circuit?"

"That's the idea." Ian didn't provide any details as he polished off the rest of his food, but Levi didn't seem like the kind of guy who wanted any.

After two whiskeys, Ian switched to beer. His eyes got heavy, his ass was already numb, and his trailer and a good night's sleep called to him.

Still, he didn't leave. He stayed in his corner of the bar, watching the crowd dance and drink and have fun. There had already been a scuffle between a couple of cowboys, but things settled down after the bartender kicked them out.

Cora's friends had left after the live band packed up, but the jukebox blared country music and the dance floor filled to capacity. After a few drinks, Cora had joined everyone on the dance floor. She danced off to one side with a few other women, having not danced with a single man all night.

"She have a boyfriend or something?" Ian asked Levi.

Levi didn't need to ask who *she* was. "No."

Short. To the point. Should have answered the question, but

the way Levi said that one word made Ian think there was a whole other story behind it. "I don't get it. She's the most beautiful woman in the room and not a single guy has asked her to dance."

"She's a living, breathing, hip-swaying hazard. Men are afraid to go near her now."

"Hazard?"

"Rumor has it she was poking holes in condoms trying to get pregnant."

Ian took a sip and grimaced at his warm beer. "You believe them?"

The guy shrugged, not as if he didn't know, but as if he didn't want to believe. "Rumors have to come from somewhere, right?"

Like all those rumors growing up that he wasn't Patrick Murphy's kid. "Maybe," Ian conceded.

The song ended and Cora and a couple of the girls she'd hooked up with headed back to her table, her arms raised and her hips swaying to the new song as she walked, stumbling her last few steps. Back at the table, she guzzled the last of her beer.

About the time another round of beer came, a new song started playing. A cheer went up from the women and everyone that had left the dance floor went back, this time lining up shoulder to shoulder under the stage lights.

Ian raised his camera and got off a couple shots. Another cheer went through the crowd, this time from the men. He lowered his camera as Cora stepped on a chair and climbed up on a row of tables that had been pushed together. Cora almost stumbled again, but someone caught her hand and helped her up.

"She's blotto. She's going to fall and break her neck." Ian didn't think 'blotto' needed translating. Anyone with eyes could see she was drunk. "You going to do something?"

Under the lights, the sparkles on her turquoise shirt flashed, and light bounced off her polished belt buckle like a beacon in a storm.

Beside him Levi grunted. "She's made it perfectly clear she's not my responsibility anymore."

Ian had suspected that Levi and Cora might have a history. Ian gave him an incredulous look. "Say that again."

Levi cussed under his breath and headed toward Cora.

Ian picked up his camera and started snapping full body pictures as Cora danced to the music. He zoomed in, taking a few shots of her face, her features shadowed and backlit.

He lowered his camera as Levi stepped up to the table, his hand outstretched trying to talk her into getting down. A man stood up beside Levi and gave him a shove.

As Ian lifted his camera and zoomed out, all hell broke loose.

———

CORA'S HEART BEAT TO THE BASS OF THE MUSIC, THE RHYTHM IN her ears, in her veins, in her soul. She closed her eyes and let the music take her far away. Someplace where the judgmental stares turned friendly and rumors weren't taken as gospel. As much as it hurt, she refused to let it show.

"Cora." Levi called her name, but she didn't want to return to reality. She clapped her hands over her head, swung her hips, and stomped her boots to the beat. "*Cora!*"

She opened her eyes. Levi stood before her, his hand outstretched.

"Go away." She had to shout to be heard over the music and the raucous calls of the men around the table.

"Get down, now." Levi had his I'm-not-kidding face on, reminding her a lot of her father. If Levi thought that would work on her, he'd forgotten who he was dealing with.

One of the men at the table stood. "You heard the lady."

Levi bowed up. Someone yanked the plug on the jukebox and the bar went silent as Levi growled low in his throat. "Sit down and shut up."

Cora stopped dancing. The man was about Levi's height, but nowhere near Levi's bulk. Levi's hands fisted at his sides as he bumped chests with the other man.

It had been months since she'd been with Levi. They'd both moved on, but right now he seemed a little too invested, a little too protective of her.

Someone in the crowd started chanting, *fight, fight, fight*. Others joined in. All she'd wanted to do was have a little fun, not cause a brawl. "Stop it. Both of you," Cora said. "I'm getting down."

Neither of the men heard her. The man challenged Levi. "You gonna make me shut up?"

"Guys, gu—"

The man shoved Levi into the table. The legs shook. Cora screamed, pinwheeling her arms. Trying to catch her balance, she stepped too close to the edge, tipping the table. As she started falling, two men grabbed Levi, pinning his arms behind his back.

In a bar fight, everyone wanted Levi on their side. But three against one were bad odds, even for a guy who wrestled six-hundred-pound steers for a living.

She landed with an *oomph*. Not from her, but from the soft-gutted guy who'd broken her fall. The bartender called out for them to break up the fight, but no one listened. Levi probably couldn't hear over the cheers from the crowd as punch after powerful punch landed in Levi's midsection.

How was Levi still standing?

She had to break the fight up before Levi got seriously hurt. Cora scrambled to her feet as Levi raged, fighting to free his arms, his face ferocious and red.

The bartender hurdled the bar with a wooden bat in his hand, and a burly man in a cook's apron right behind him. *Hurry.* Cora's breath came quick and her heart galloped in her chest.

She grabbed a chair by the legs, swinging it above her head. Someone shoved her down. She crashed onto her knee. Pain shot up her leg and she crumbled, the smell of spilled beer filled her nose and the peanut shells on the floor crunched under her weight.

Then the guy in the bell bottom jeans who had pushed her out of harm's way, yanked one of the men off Levi, landing a punch to the guy's jaw and dropping Levi's attacker like a stone.

With a roar, Levi broke free from the other man's grasp and rushed the man who'd restrained him, taking the guy to the ground in a pile of arms and legs, grunts and groans.

The bartender and the cook fought through the crowd and pulled the men apart. The cook stood with his arms outstretched, a palm on Levi's and the other man's chest. The bartender pointed his bat at the man Levi had been fighting and said, "Matty, get your boys and get the hell out of here before I call the cops."

Matty spat blood on the ground, his eyes going back to Levi. The bartender stepped into Matty's line of sight. "Try me, asshole."

Shifting his eyes to the bartender, Matty took a step back. Levi didn't relax until the guy bent and picked up his hat and said to his friends, "Let's go, boys."

To the rest of the bar's patrons the bartender said, "That's it. We're closed. Everyone pay up and go home."

A chorus of complaints went up, but the crowd started to disperse. Levi stepped over and offered Cora a hand, helping her to her feet. She hissed in a breath as her weight shifted to her knee and she almost went down again.

"You okay?" Levi asked.

"I'm—" She was going to say 'fine', but then she glanced up at Levi's face, at his left eye that was already starting to swell and the dribble of blood at the corner of his mouth. "Better than you."

He'd always been reserved and slow to smile. There'd been a darkness to him when they'd dated. Not as if he was dangerous, but as if he couldn't allow himself to have any fun.

"Sorry," she said. "This was all my fault."

His eyes locked on hers for a beat then he cracked a small smile. "It's okay. I needed to let off some steam."

Levi righted the table and headed toward the back hall and the restrooms, as she found her hat and hobbled to the bar and paid her and Levi's tabs. By the time she finished, the bar had cleared out except for her, Levi, and a guy packing a camera into a bag at the end of the bar.

To him she said, "Maybe I should pay your tab as well."

The man glanced up. His right cheek sported a scuff, his knuckles were bloodied and there was a rip in his shirt where the sleeve met the shoulder. "You don't owe me anything."

"You're the one who helped Levi. If it hadn't been for me—" she cut herself off before her voice cracked and she started crying like a little kid. He was a stranger, yet he'd stepped in while others had stood back and cheered. She swallowed hard. "Why'd you do it?"

He zipped up his bag and tossed back the last of his drink. "It wasn't a fair fight."

Levi returned, the blood washed from his face. He stuck out his hand to the man. "I owe you one, brother."

"You know him?" Cora asked.

Levi glanced at the man as if deciding what to say. "We shared a drink," was what Levi went with.

The man held out his hand to her. "Ian Murphy." Before she could say anything else, he added, "I'm from up north."

"No kidding."

Levi tapped the bar and said, "I'm outta here."

"You need a ride?" Cora asked.

"It's not far. The walk will do me good."

The bartender cleared the bar top of empty bottles and dirty glasses, the beer bottles breaking and shattering as he tossed them into the trash bin. Ian shouldered his bag and came around the end of the bar.

"Why weren't you surprised I'm from up north?"

She fell into step beside him as they headed for the door. "The New York accent for one."

Ian got to the door first and held it open for her, her knee bitching and complaining and generally making her regret ever letting Josephine talk her into going out. The cold wind slammed into her, biting through her clothes. She hadn't bothered with her jacket because she hadn't wanted to lose track of it at the bar.

"What's the other?" He asked.

"The other what?"

"The other reason you knew I wasn't from around here."

"This is me," she said as she stopped at Josephine's truck and unlocked the door. She waved her hand up and down his body. "Your clothes."

He glanced down at himself. "That's what I've been told. What's bloody wrong with my clothes?"

"I know it's the fashion, but no one down here wears bell bottom jeans, and we wear leather boots, not loafers. We have belts with large buckles, and that button up shirt reminds me of something a city slicker would wear to a board meeting."

"Ouch," he said, though the smile spread over his face.

"You asked," she said. "I'm not judging."

"Fair enough." When a shiver went through her, he pointed at the truck. "Better get in before you freeze to death."

She climbed in and he closed the door behind her. She rolled down her window, the wind nipped at her nose as it whistled in.

"You okay to drive?" He asked.

"Yeah. I think that spike of adrenaline sobered me up." She put the key in the ignition and went to depress the clutch. Pain shot up her leg, and she cried out.

"What's wrong?"

She grabbed at her knee, but it did nothing to ease the pain. Her stomach dropped. She wouldn't have to worry about knocking down the barrels if she couldn't even ride. "My knee. I can't work the clutch."

He popped open her door. "Come on, I'll give you a ride to where ever you need to go."

She hesitated. She didn't really know this guy. Sure, he helped Levi, and he was easy on the eyes, but before tonight, she'd never seen him around before. He could be a serial killer or—

"I promise I'm not an ax-murderer."

She offered a wary smile. "I'm pretty sure that's what all the ax-murderers say."

He held out his hand. "Come on, I'm freezing my nuts off out here."

Oh yeah, her eyes went straight to his crotch. In her defense, it was near enough to eye level to not be blatantly obvious. She hoped. *You need to get laid.* Josephine's words echoed in her brain. Too bad Cora only slept with cowboys.

And non-serial killers.

But it was either accept the ride or she'd have to walk. She glanced around. The cook and the bartender were locking up, and there was no sign of a pay phone out front.

He raised a brow at her and she finally took his hand and let him help her out of the truck. She rolled up the window and locked the door. They walked to his truck and he handed her into the passenger seat.

When he climbed in on the other side, she said, "I have a black belt in karate so don't try—"

He busted out a laugh as he dropped his bag on the floorboards by her feet. He looked her up and down. "You don't know karate."

"How do you know?"

He held her gaze. She swallowed hard. When he looked at her like that, it made her feel vulnerable, like he could see deep down at all that she was and—more frightening—all that she could never be. "You don't have killer eyes."

"I do too." She didn't have to force the indignation. She could look dangerous if she wanted to. She narrowed her eyes at him and gave him *the look.*

He chuckled, his eyes going bright. "Lass, the only thing you're going to slay with those eyes is someone's heart."

The breath she blew came out as a vapor cloud. "Okay. You're right. I never took karate. But I once shoved a kid in fifth grade when he wouldn't let me climb on the old tractor tires on the playground at recess."

Ian's grin got wider, and her stomach did a belly flop. He really did have the most amazing smile. The amusement lingered in his eyes. "Duly noted. You get first dibs on tractor tires."

The starter cranked and cranked before it caught and roared to life. "Where to?" Ian asked.

"The rodeo grounds, it's—"

Somehow, his grin got even grinnier. "I know where it is. That's where I'm headed, as well."

"*You're* a cowboy?" The incredulity pitched her voice high enough that he might have taken it as an insult. She expected his smile to slip, but it didn't.

"Even better." His smile said he was about to surprise her with an incredible gift. "I'm a photographer."

3

IAN HADN'T EXPECTED TO GO THROUGH THE WHOLE EXPLANATION as to what he was doing at the rodeo and why, but if he was going to fit in, if he was going to be trusted, he couldn't lie from the start.

On the way back to the rodeo grounds, he gave Cora the grainy, black and white, low light, quick-snap version of leaving home, about his dream of the future, of traveling the world. It sounded silly, and idealistic, and frankly unachievable when he voiced it out loud.

No wonder his Da had laughed in his face.

He pulled into the parking lot, half expecting Cora to laugh as well. She had such a full-color, Kodachrome laugh, he almost wouldn't mind if she did.

But she didn't.

"That's amazing. Your parents must be really proud of you."

Amazing. Proud. He had to laugh. "Hardly."

She got a look on her face and for a second there, he thought she would make him explain. She pointed. "That's me over there."

He pulled to a stop in front of a trailer. The back section of the trailer had horizontal slats open to the air, for hauling horses he suspected, and what looked like a small enclosed area in the front. Including the horse compartment, the length was shorter than his camper. How did she fit in there to sleep?

He threw the truck into Park. "Seriously? This is where you live?"

"What's wrong with it?"

"Nothing. There just doesn't seem to be a lot of room."

She popped the door. "We make it work."

We? Now he *had* to see this.

He climbed out, and over the roof of his truck she said, "Where are you going?"

"I want a tour."

"It's after midnight."

"Humor me. It's not like it will take long." He didn't know why he pushed. It wasn't like he really cared what the inside of her trailer looked like. He just didn't want the night to end.

She studied him a moment, the overhead street light was at her back, throwing shadows over her face. "Fine." She took a step and with a muffled cry, grabbed onto his side mirror to keep from going to her knees.

He ran over and took her hand, helping her to stand. "I thought you said your knee was okay."

"It was. It is. I mean—" she hissed as she tried to take another step, the pain twisting up her pretty face. "It must have stiffened up from the cold."

He put her arm around his shoulder and he held her around her waist. "Put your weight on me."

Together, she hopped-hobbled to her trailer, and only pulled her arm from around his shoulder to get the key out of her pocket. He helped her inside. All his life, he'd never considered how a sardine felt packed in a can, but now he knew. There was hardly enough room for the both of them to stand.

Cora clicked on a battery powered lantern and shined the light up. Standing straight, Ian's head almost brushed the metal ceiling. On the wall between the front and rear, there were two bunks attached to the wall. To his right, someone had rigged a clothes rod. In the nose of the trailer were two folding camping chairs, with four plastic milk crates stacked between them two by two.

Light from the pole outside shined through the front window that followed the curve of the trailer's nose. Cora eased herself onto the bottom bunk and let out a soft groan. Ian tried to ignore it. She was groaning from pain, not pleasure, but he'd be hard pressed telling that to his dick.

Ian pushed that thought from his mind. Like he'd told Levi, he wasn't here for sex. He was here to make his career.

Cora stuck her leg up in the air, her booted foot at his waist. "Pull. I can't bend my knee to get it off."

He gave her boot a yank and tossed it in a corner. He grabbed the other one and did the same.

"Thanks." She pointed to the stack of milk crates. "Can you toss me an extra pair of socks, so my feet don't freeze tonight?"

He found a pair but didn't bother handing them over. If she couldn't get her boots off, she wouldn't be able to get the socks on. "Gimme your feet, lass."

This time she did laugh at him. It was full and fun, and it warmed his chest instead of lighting his temper.

"Lass?"

"Sorry." He flattened out his accent. "My parents were Irish immigrants. As much as I try to keep it in check, it tends to slip out when I'm tired or have been drinking. I'll have to practice saying *darlin'* with a drawl."

"Don't. I kinda like it."

"You do?"

"I do."

He motioned for her to give him her feet, feeling like a bloody fool that the smile he couldn't smother made his cheeks ache. She braced the soles of her feet against his stomach as he slipped the extra pair of socks on one by one.

His thumb brushed across her instep and her head fell back and a soft moan tumbled from her lips. He pressed harder into her arches, and it took everything he had not to drop his voice a register and say, 'What else do you like, Cora Hayes?'

As he massaged her foot, she lifted her head. Shadows covered her face, but in the quiet of the trailer he couldn't miss the hitch in her breath or the way her tongue slid across her bottom lip.

He dropped her foot. He couldn't tell if she was glad or mad as she scooted her legs onto the bunk. Didn't matter. He was here to do a job, not her. "You have any ice for that knee?"

Stupid question.

She glanced around. "I seem to be fresh out. But I'm okay. I'm sure it will be feeling better in the morning."

"Fine," he said, though he didn't agree. "Where's your heater? I'll turn it on before I go."

"No heater." Cora reached for a blanket at the foot of the bunk and pulled the covers over the top of her.

He tapped at the thermometer stuck to her wall. "It's literally freezing in here." Then he pointed to the front window, at the condensation that had built from their combined breath and the way it had crystallized on the glass. "There are icicles forming on the *inside*."

"It'll be fine. Cowgirls are tough. We don't melt in the rain, or shrivel up in the heat, or freeze in the cold. If I bury my head under the covers, I won't even shiver much."

He stared her, his hands on his waist. "You've got to be freaking kidding me." She couldn't stay here. He yanked the covers off her. It wouldn't do any good to give her a choice.

"Hey!" She grabbed for the blankets. "I'm gonna lose all my heat."

He took her hand and pulled her to her feet. "You don't need it. You're coming to my trailer. I have a real mattress and a heater. I don't want to find out you froze to death in the middle of the night."

Her face scrunched up and he could tell she was about to argue when she sighed. "You win. But only because I'm tired, and my head hurts, and I hate being cold."

"Thank you." He laughed to himself. How did *he* end up thanking *her*?

In the end, he gave her a piggy-back ride over to his camper to keep her off her sore leg. Once inside, he dumped her at the end of the U-shaped bench seat that wrapped around the kitchen table at the front of his camper. He dropped his camera bag at the other end. The dirty plate and empty chip bag he shoved to the far side of the table.

"Sorry about the mess. I wasn't expecting company." He fiddled with the thermostat until it clicked and the blower for his propane heater turned on. He blew into his hands, trying to relieve the cold and stiffness. He pointed to the back of the trailer where he had a full-size bed. "You can sleep there. I don't have a change of sheets, but I've only been on the road a few nights, so they shouldn't be too hideous."

The kitchen lined the wall opposite the door. Propane stove, sink, counter with gas refrigerator underneath. "Help yourself to whatever is in the fridge." He pointed to a sliding door across from the sink. "Bathroom's there."

Cora stood and limped over to him, using the counter to help keep her weight off her leg. "I really appreciate this. I'll get out of your hair first thing in the morning. I promise."

"No rush. You're welcome here as long as you'd like."

"You're very sweet," she said as she worked her way to the bed. She sat on the edge, but didn't get in.

"What's wrong?" he asked.

"I don't want to get spilled beer and peanut shell bits on your sheets, and my pajamas are back at my trailer."

Ian stared at the door the same way Cora did, as if they could will her pajamas to appear. Regrettably, they couldn't. It was late, he had a ton of work to do, and he was just now starting to thaw out.

"How about I lend you a T-shirt to sleep in for the night?"

She hesitated, clearly uncomfortable with the idea. Of course, she would be. They were practically strangers.

"Never mind," he said. "Stay in your clothes. You aren't going to ruin the sheets."

"No. It's okay. A shirt would be nice if that's all right with you."

He dug through one of the drawers under the bed, pulled out an old Mets T-shirt, and handed it to her. Her fingers brushed his and the blood in his veins warmed. "I'll...um..." He pointed to the front of the trailer. "I'll be over there. I won't look. I promise."

Her eyes had a mischievous glint. She knew exactly where his mind had gone, and she didn't seem put off by it. Damn good thing she only went after cowboys.

She smiled, and before he thought of a way to prove to her all the creative ways that photographers were better than cowboys, he moved to the other end of the trailer.

He turned on the light over the table and dug out the rolls of film he'd taken on the trip down. He'd burned through more rolls than he'd planned, but it had been his first time through the Smokey Mountains, and his first time that far from home, so he'd gotten carried away. He'd have to be more selective if his film supply was going to last. From the back of the camera, he stripped the roll he'd used up at the bar. More eager than he should have been to enlarge the shots he'd taken of Cora.

Behind him, Cora grunted and cussed as she struggled out of her jeans with her bum knee. He heard her clothes hit the linoleum as well as the shuffle of the sheets as she slid in. As tempted as he was to peek, he didn't dare.

He wasn't that much of a prick.

Besides, they'd built a fragile trust. He'd successfully navigated past the serial killer phase and if he was going to succeed at fitting in on the circuit, he couldn't risk crushing his credibility.

"Okay," she said at last. "I'm decent."

He turned to see her lying in his bed. The thick blanket covered her up to her neck. It shouldn't have been sexy, but with her long hair spilling out over his pillow and knowing full well what she was—and more importantly, wasn't wearing—made him harder.

He turned back toward the table and adjusted himself. "Is this light going to keep you up?"

"You're not coming to bed?" Her face scrunched up and that riotous laugh he liked so much filled the inside of the camper. "That came out all wrong. I didn't mean 'bed' as in we're sleeping together."

He stared at her a moment too long and she must have thought he misunderstood because she quickly added, "I meant 'bed' as in I sleep on this side and you sleep way over there on the other side in a strictly platonic, no sex kind of way. It's your trailer. I don't want you sleeping on the cold floor."

"I knew what you meant. And no. I'm not going to bed. I've got a bunch of work to do. If I get too tired I can crash over here. The table folds down and makes a bed."

"Suit yourself." She fluffed up his pillow and snuggled into it, her eyes drifting closed. He'd gathered up the rolls of film and had slid open the door to his bathroom-turned-darkroom when she asked, "Why are you being so nice to me?"

He glanced over. Cora's eyes had gone soft and half-mast, her lashes brushing her cheek. She looked warm and cozy. The mountain of blankets did nothing to hide her sensuality. Ian wanted to reach for his camera, wanted to immortalize this moment. "Can't a guy be nice?"

"In my experience, there's usually an ulterior motive."

Before he proved her right, before he did something stupid and crawled into bed with her, he said, "Get some sleep."

By the time he'd prepped the dark room for developing, her eyes had drifted closed and her breathing had evened out. He closed the bathroom door behind him, turned on the red light, and stuffed an old towel under the door to protect the rolls of film as he stripped the negatives out of their plastic housings.

There was something he wanted from her, and tomorrow he'd have to tell Cora the truth.

———

Cora woke to the sun streaming through the dirty window of Ian's camper, and the stomach-grumbling pop and snap of bacon frying.

She groaned and stretched. "Something smells good."

"Bacon's almost done," Ian said, his voice gravelly that early in the morning. She ignored the delicious way that rumble raised the goosebumps on her arms. "Scrambled eggs okay?"

"Perfect." She leaned over the edge of the bed and retrieved her jeans. "Please tell me that's coffee I smell."

"Instant, but yeah."

She pulled her pants under the sheets and struggled to get them on. She was out of breath by the time she put her feet on the cold floor. Her knee twinged.

"How's the leg?"

"Sore. Better though."

He took a sip of his coffee and she stole it out of his hands. "Help yourself," he said, the slow smile sliding across his face.

She drank some down and handed it back. "Just enough to tide me over until I can make one of my own. She pointed to the bathroom. "Do you mind?"

"Ahh..." His eyes darted toward the closed door and he shifted from foot to foot, looking like a kid who'd got caught looking at Playboy. "Give me a sec."

He shut off the burner and disappeared into the bathroom, closing the door firmly behind him. Cora leaned against the counter and plucked a piece of bacon out of the pan. *Hot. Hot. Hot.* It scalded. She quickly chewed and swallowed it down. Best hangover food *ever*.

Inside the bathroom, Ian thumped around, a cabinet door banged closed and then another. Cora crossed her legs. She really, really, *really* had to pee. "You almost done in there?"

The bathroom door slid open and Ian stepped out with several stuffed manila folders held against his chest. "All yours," he said as he dumped the folders on the dining table.

Inside his bathroom, he'd strung multiple rows of clothes line between the shower walls and had three deep trays of liquid on the shower pan. A chemical smell burned her nose and an eerie red light bathed the bathroom, reminding her of the set of a horror movie. "Is this your idea of mood lighting, Ian? It looks like a bordello in here. Or are those trays of chemicals how you dissolve your victims?"

Ian rushed over and turned off the red light and switched on the overhead light. "Sorry. The bathroom doubles as my darkroom, not as my way to dispose of the dead bodies. I'd need a lot more room for that. Good thing my camper is small and you're too cute to kill."

"Funny."

She closed the door and used his facilities unable to get the 'you're too cute' part out of her head. Turning on the faucet she splashed water on her face, appreciating not having to go out in the cold to clean up. Who was she kidding? With how low the temps had dropped the night before, all of her jugs of water had to be frozen solid by now.

She came out to find Ian sitting at the table, with a couple mugs of coffee and two plates of food going cold. "You didn't have to wait for me."

He picked up his fork as she sat and picked up hers. "My ma did manage to beat a few manners into me."

"Speaking of beating..." She pointed with her fork at the bruising and scuff mark on his cheek. "You didn't do too bad out there for a city slicker. How's the face."

"Fine. When I was a kid, my brothers routinely did worse damage before breakfast. This is nothing."

"That's where you learned to fight?"

Something dark flashed in his eyes, but then his expression softened, and he shrugged like it didn't matter. Cora didn't buy it.

"Do or die. Right?" he said.

She studied him, not taking her eyes off his as she reached for her coffee, knocking it over. "Sorry." Cora scrambled to her feet and grabbed for the folders trying to save them from the river of coffee flowing their way. "I'm such a klutz."

Ian went for a rag as photographs slipped from the folders and fell onto the floor. Cora ignored the pain in her leg as she got on her hands and knees beneath the table. "Quick, toss me a rag."

He slapped one in her hand and used one of his own to wipe the top of the table. More coffee splattered onto the floor and she sopped it up, gathering up the three photos that had fallen face down. She dabbed at the coffee that had landed on the backs of the pictures.

"You need another rag?" Ian asked.

"I think I'm good." She scooted out from beneath the table.

Ian's eyes went round and he snatched the photos out of her hand. He didn't even bother checking to make sure there wasn't any liquid on the front of them before shoving them back into one of the manila folders.

Her stomach rolled over and it had nothing to do with the fact she'd had too much to drink the night before. What was up with the photos?

Ian sat back down and tucked back into his food, unwilling to meet her eye. "Eat before it gets cold."

Cora sat, though for the first time since they'd met, a tickle of unease gnawed in her gut. She didn't take him for a serial killer, or even dangerous. If she had, she never would have been sitting there, much less spent the night there. The fact that he hadn't tried to make a pass supported her instincts.

But not being dangerous didn't mean he wasn't hiding something.

The silence grew oppressive as they ate, until her gut was so knotted she couldn't force another bite. She pushed her half-eaten meal away. "Did I do something wrong?"

Ian pushed the eggs around on his plate. "No. It's fine." Instead of looking up at her, his gaze landed on the manila folder. What didn't he want her to see? She reached for the folder, but he beat her to it and slid it to his side of the table.

"Why can't I see the pictures?"

"I'm protective of my work."

She held out her hand and wiggled her fingers at him, not really expecting he would let her see them, but determined to try. "Let me see."

He picked up the folders, indecision warring in his green

eyes. Then he held it out to her. She took hold, but he didn't let them go.

"What?" she asked.

"Just..." He sighed and shook his head. "It's not what it looks like."

Still he didn't let go.

What could be so bad that he didn't want her to see? The hairs on the back of her neck stood up one by one and she suppressed the shiver. "Did you sneak pictures of me while I was changing last night?"

He sat up straight. "What? No." Still, he had that hand-caught-in-the-cookie-jar look on his face.

"Is it pornography?"

His face softened. He almost smiled. "No."

She gave the folder a little tug. "Then let me see."

Finally, he relented. His color went pale then shifted to light green as if he might get sick. She pushed her plate aside and he busied himself by clearing the table and cleaning up. She flipped through the photos. Scenery shots. Mountains and Magnolias and morning mist. Sun and moon and long ribbons of road. Every shot more stunning than the last.

She glanced up at him as he leaned back against the counter, an arm over his chest, his chin in his hand as he watched her reactions. "These..." She didn't have the words to describe how the photographs made her feel.

But it was more than just a feeling. Through his photographs, she saw the world through his eyes, like peeping through a crack in the door and seeing his soul. "I don't think I'll ever look at a rusted out old truck the same way again. It's...beautiful. The lines, the light, the..."

Ian lowered his arms and rested his hands on the counter behind him, a grimace on his face.

"Why would you have a problem with me seeing these? They're extraordinary."

His knuckles got white as he gripped the counter and the pulse at the base of his neck thrummed. He cleared his throat. "Keep going."

She thumbed through a couple more photographs, then one of them stuck to the photograph below it. With care, she peeled them apart. It took her a few seconds before what she saw registered. "Ohmygod."

4

IAN RUSHED OVER AND SLID INTO THE SEAT ACROSS FROM CORA, her hair still adorably sleep-tousled and her makeup smudged. "It's not what you think."

"I don't know what to say."

Ian didn't know if she'd whispered her words or if it was the blood rushing past his ears that made her difficult to hear. "I can explain."

She glanced up at him, her expression unreadable. He couldn't blow this. He didn't have the time or the money to find another circuit to follow if all this went to shit. But when he opened his mouth to speak, the words wouldn't flow. They stuck on the back of his tongue nearly choking him.

Looking back down at the photo, Cora ran a light finger over her image. "Is this the way you saw me?" Awe coated her words, not anger. When she glanced back up at him it was with wonder, not wrath.

He scooted around to her side of the table and she slid over to accommodate him. "When you climbed up on that table, I just knew I had to capture the...the..."

"Essence?" Cora supplied.

Cora's blue eyes met his. They were the clear blue of a summer sky at dawn. When had he ever seen such warmth, such understanding staring back at him? "Exactly." He glanced at her mouth, at the way her tongue traced her bottom lip.

Don't you dare kiss her.

He leaned away. He didn't want her to think he was a pervert. He scratched at the stubble on his jaw. After three days on the road, he desperately needed a shave.

She still held the picture in her hand. In the shot, he'd caught her with her hands above her head, her head down as the moves and the music touched her. In the background behind her, the shutter had snapped as someone's fist connected with Levi's face. A cowboy hat forever hanging in mid-air.

Her eyes roved all over as if taking in every minute detail. "I like how the darkness plays against the light. How the innocence of the dancing contrasts with the brutality of the fight."

She ran her finger over the curve of her hip, the exact spot where he'd like to lay his hand. "I look so uninhibited, so fun, so free."

So beautiful. "What were you thinking when that shot was taken?"

A soft laugh huffed out of her mouth. "Everything and nothing. My mind closed off to the world except for the music. I let the beat and the beer take me away."

"Y-you're not mad?" He thought he knew the answer, but he needed to hear it from her mouth to be certain.

She put a hand over his and gave it a light squeeze before pulling away. Sparks didn't fly when they touched, but his heart gave his sternum a swift kick as if telling his body that it had better pay attention. His blood warmed in his veins, spreading throughout his chest. The skin on the back of his hand still holding the imprint of her touch.

He would like to think he would wash that hand again some-time, but he wasn't making any promises.

She flipped through the rest of the photographs, then took the stack and tapped it on the table, straightening them out and handing them back to him. "You have an amazing talent. A gift even. That magazine you want to work for would be insane not to pick you."

He smiled for the first time since she picked up the photographs. "Great. Now all I have to do is get the shots I need and wow the magazine editor like I did you. I just gotta find a way to fit in, or at the very least blend into the background."

She leaned away and looked him up and down, her eye critical. "You're never gonna blend in dressed like that."

Again, with the clothes. He held his hands up. "This was the best I could do. I'm not a rodeo fashion expert."

"Clearly," she said, the amused, calculating smile taking the sting out of her words. "If you're looking for your personal fashion expert, you've come to the right place."

"You?" He didn't dare tell her he'd been about to ask her for that very help. He'd let her think it had been her bright idea.

"I've been in rodeo all my life. If anyone can make you look like you fit in, it's me." She nudged his shoulder and he moved to let her out of the booth.

"I've gotta go take care of my horse," she said. "Meet me back at my trailer in an hour."

She still had socks on her feet, but her trailer was close, so he let her go. The door was almost closed when he called out. "What if I had other plans?"

Turning back, she stuck her head through the doorway. "Change them."

———

AS THE LARGEST NEWSPAPER IN TOWN, IAN TARGETED *THE EL PASO Tribune* as his best shot at an editor paying a decent rate for one of his photographs.

It was a long shot, though. Many of the larger papers had their own photographers on staff and buying from a freelancer wasn't necessarily the norm. But after spending most of the day shopping with Cora, he'd blown what little money he'd had left.

He waited outside the editor's office, his new leather cowboy boots tight across the balls of his feet. Cora assured him they would stretch. The *rat-a-tat-tat* of the typewriters buzzed along. Phones rang non-stop and the hub-bub of all the voices nearly deafened him.

He placed his new black Stetson on the wood bench beside him and ran a hand through his hair, having a hard time getting used to the feel of the short haircut that she'd insisted would make him look less like a city hippie.

If he'd had any balls, he'd have reined in his spending, but she was having too much fun, and he'd enjoyed her company too much for him to cut the shopping short.

Now he was paying for thinking with his ego and his dick.

A door down the hall opened and a tall slender man with short-cropped white hair stuck his head out. "Mr. Murphy?"

"That's me." Ian gathered up his hat and folder of photos and walked down the hall, the unfamiliar clump of his boots tagging along. He stuck out his hand as he greeted the man. "Thanks for seeing me, Mr. Hakes."

Hakes gave his hand an abbreviated shake as if he couldn't spare the extra time to give it two good pumps. Hakes fell into his chair behind his desk and pointed to the one across from him. "Have a seat. I'm on a tight deadline. You've got five minutes."

Ian explained who he was and that he hoped to sell some photos. With the shopping trip taking up most of the day, he hadn't had any time to take any behind the scenes shots at the rodeo grounds that day, so he'd brought what he'd developed the night before. With the biggest day of the rodeo weekend coming up the next day, he didn't even have a good photo to sell for tomorrow's Sunday edition.

Except the ones he'd taken of Cora. He hadn't even brought those.

Hakes held out his hand for Ian's folder and leaned back in his squeaky chair. One by one he flipped through the photographs. Selecting several and laying them out on top of his tidy desk. His office wasn't the cluttered, paper-filled mess that Ian had expected. Even the books in the case against the wall were neatly ordered by size and color of spine.

At the last photo, Ian's breath caught. There were two photos stuck together. He reached across the desk wanting to take them back and separate them. "Sorry, one got stuck. That one wasn't supposed to be there."

Instead of handing over the pictures, Hakes separated them himself. Ian groaned when Hake's appreciative eyes locked on Cora. The man probably couldn't identify her even if he knew her, not with her face in the shadows like they were. But still. *He* knew.

"When was this taken?" No question Hake's was asking about the one of Cora, not the rusted out pickup truck.

"Late last night at The Wagon Wheel."

Hakes dropped Cora's photo on top of his desk with three others. A derelict oil derrick, a herd of tumbleweeds blowing across an old two-lane road Ian had gotten lost on, and a Welcome to El Paso sign.

The editor gave him a price for all four. A respectable price. Ian would be stupid not to take the money. As it was, he'd be lucky to get back to the rodeo grounds with his tank and his wallet on empty.

"The Wagon Wheel isn't for sale."

Hakes studied him...and studied him. Ian stared back. Staring was easy. The editor's eyes didn't hold the hatred his father's always had.

"All or nothing," the man said.

Leaning forward, Ian started gathering all the photos even as his brain kept telling him to take the offer. "Sorry I wasted your time."

Hakes laid a staying hand on the folder. "I'll double it."

What's the big deal? No one can tell it's her. Don't be an idiot. Take the damn money.

If he didn't do anything stupid, the cash would keep him in gas and food for a couple of weeks at least.

Hakes glanced at the clock on the wall. "I don't have all day."

You want to push your truck back to the rodeo grounds?

"Deal," Ian said as the macaroni and cheese he'd had at lunch curdled in his stomach.

Hakes filled out a receipt and pointed across the room to a young woman who sat at a corner desk. "Take this to Irene. She'll pay you."

Ian stood to shake the man's hand. "Thank you."

Bobbing his chin at the Wagon Wheel photo, he said, "You have any more like that one, I'll buy those too."

He had more of those. More than he'd like to admit. "Sorry. That's all I've got."

Ian left the *Tribune* office with a pocket full of cash. The guilt threatened to overpower the pride he felt over someone else valuing his work. He should have felt on top of the world, like he could rescue damsels in distress and slay dragons, but with Cora's photo in that pile he sold, he felt cheap and dirty.

———

THE COLD RAYS OF WINTER SUN WEREN'T POWERFUL ENOUGH TO burn off the low bank of clouds Cora saw through the window of her trailer early Sunday morning. She snuck a hand out from under her blanket and got a few aspirin from the bottle she'd left by her bunk.

Her knee had improved. She'd been able to ride the night before, and had managed not to drop a barrel, qualifying her for the last slot to run for the money in the races that night. But spending the night in the freezing cold trailer had made her knee stiff and sore again.

At least with Josephine spending her nights at the motel with Silas, Cora could use the lower bunk and not have to jump down from the top one.

She dressed in extra layers and cracked open the door. The wind had died down leaving a heavy gray sky in its place. As she went to step down, she caught herself. A copy of the *El Paso Tribune* lay on her step, a rock over the top to keep the paper from blowing away.

Along with another red rose.

What the? She glanced around. In the distance someone walked into the barn, but they paid her no attention. She unfolded the paper, her eye immediately going to the photo on the front page.

The photo of her.

"Ian!" she screeched out, not caring who she woke at that early hour. She stormed over to his trailer, seeing red, and magenta and crimson, and every other color in the *Pissed Off* hue. After everything she'd done for him the day before, *this* is how he paid her back?

She pounded Ian's door with the meat of her fist. "Ian, you sad sonofabitch, open up."

Bam, bam, bam, bam. She pounded again and again. Caddo

O'Shea who'd slept in his truck a couple spots over rolled down his window and told her to keep it down.

"Ian. Open this damn door or I'll—"

The door flung open. Ian stood in the doorway, his hair wet, his chest bare, and a towel wrapped around his waist. She barged up the steps not waiting for an embossed, engraved or any other kind of invitation.

"Mind telling me what the hell is going on?" he asked.

"What's going on? *What's going on?* Are you kidding me?"

"Cora—"

She slapped the paper to his chest. He caught it before it hit the ground. "Care to explain that to me?"

Above the fold in bold font was the headline: *Rowdy Rodeo.* Beneath that it read: *Critics say the cash isn't worth the cost.* But that wasn't what Cora had wanted him to see. Below that, before the article itself, was the photo from The Wagon Wheel.

He blew out a breath, but before he could speak, she held up a staying hand and started pacing back and forth—which proved difficult in such a confined space. "Don't even start."

She made several passes. "I'm pissed."

"I can see that."

She made several more trips, then glance up and shot him a look of exasperation. "Why are you looking at me like that?"

"Like what?" He sounded innocent. Cora knew he wasn't.

"Like you're itching to grab your camera and start snapping pictures."

"Guilty."

He didn't look it.

She stopped pacing for a moment, anger giving way to intrigue into how his mind worked. She hadn't ever cared too much about what a man thought before. A simple hookup didn't require a connection past the physical.

"What makes you want to do that?"

He blinked at her and she could almost hear his mental gears grind as his mind caught up with her question. Then his eyes lit, and passion flooded in. Not for her. For photography.

"It's your energy," he said. The emotion. It's captivating. You don't have to speak when your body language does it for you. The tight way you've wrapped your arms around yourself for protection, yet your fists are clenched, ready to fight."

She glanced down at her crossed arms and white knuckles.

"If I were photographing you, I'd take the shot from the ground up. You'd look larger than life, and warrior fierce. Not a victim. A tornado. A force to reckon with."

Wow. She leaned against the bathroom wall. Fisting her hair in her hands, her mind at war with her conflicting emotions. How can she be so angry and yet fascinated at the same time? "You got a beer or something?"

"It's seven in the morning."

"So?"

"Isn't that what got you into this mess to begin with?"

"No," she said. "You're what got me into this mess."

He took her by the shoulders and walked her to the table. "Sit. I'll fix you something to eat and we can talk it out. Deal?"

Cora sat, and squeezed her head between her hands. If her father saw that picture...She groaned. There was no question of *if*. Just a matter of *when*. The rodeo would swing through Corpus Christi, Texas in a couple weeks. Practically in her father's back yard. Mentally, she'd have to prepare for him to come knocking at her door.

Not that she had ever been able to adequately prepare for that kind of mental beat down.

"What's the matter?" Ian stirred instant coffee into a mug of hot water and set it on the table in front of her. While she'd been lost in thought he'd shucked the towel and pulled on a pair of jeans, though he hadn't bothered with a shirt.

Her stomach did that tumbly, fumbly thing it always did when confronted with hot man chest. She averted her gaze, she didn't want to want him. Not just because he wasn't a cowboy, but because she could already tell he wasn't like the other men. He had depth. An emotional maturity. He was someone she could see herself with if she did relationships, which she absolutely didn't.

To answer his question, she said, "My father's going to flip when he finds out."

"How is he going to find out? No one can even tell it's you."

"Whoever left the paper and the rose on my step recognized me."

Ian stopped flipping the bacon. "Rose? What rose?"

Cora waved a dismissive hand at him. "My best friend, Josephine thinks I have a secret admirer. It's nothing."

"It's creepy."

"That's not the point. *The point is* someone recognized me. Even though my parents live a couple hundred miles away in the Texas Hill Country, the rodeo crowd is tight knit. He's gonna hear about it. Maybe not today or tomorrow. But he will."

"Want me to call him and explain?" Ian placed the cooked bacon on some paper towels to drain and started beating the eggs.

"God, no." Cora pinched the bridge of her nose, the headache coming on fast. "No, he doesn't need the guy I'm sleeping with calling to explain anything."

Ian stilled mid-stroke. "We're not sleeping together."

"Doesn't matter. Between my reputation and my preacher father, you call him, and he'll make the assumption."

If Ian had thought *what reputation?* he didn't voice it. Instead, the egg mixture sizzled as Ian poured it into the pan. "He's got a rather low opinion of his daughter if you ask me."

"It's not unjustified."

She should have been ashamed to admit that, but she wasn't. Ian might not know about her reputation, but if he hung around the rodeos he'd find out soon enough. Life on the circuit could be an open book, all dog-eared, torn-pages, with scribbled notes in the margin for everyone to pick up and pass on.

Ian plated the food and joined her at the table. "You're an adult. Your personal life is no one's business but your own."

He sounded sincere. But during her time on the circuit, she'd become a quick study of men. Around a bite of bacon, she said, "That's what guys say when they're trying to talk women into sex. I know I have a reputation, but I'm not going to sleep with you."

"I'm not looking to have sex." If he was lying he was doing a damn fine job of hiding it.

Ouch. Cora then thought about all the guys who were treating her like Typhoid Mary as if her pregnancy scare was a life-threatening contagion. She muttered, "Yeah. You and everybody—or should I say nobody—else."

"What's that?"

Don't feel sorry for yourself. You're a big girl. You made your bed, now you can sleep in it...alone. "Nothing."

"Can't we just be friends? I think we could both use one right now." He held his hand out like he wanted her to shake on it.

She didn't think that's how friendships worked, but hey, she didn't have anything to lose, so she shook his hand. Then he explained how the newspaper ended up with her picture.

"If you didn't have the money, you should have told me. We didn't have to keep shopping."

"No guy wants to tell a pretty lady that he's broke."

"Pretty lady?" She cut him a look. "That doesn't sound like an uninterested friend talking."

"That wasn't a come on. I'm just stating a fact."

They fell into silence as they finished up their meal. Ian

pushed his plate away. "Look, I apologize. Selling that picture was a shitty thing to do. Being out of money is no excuse. If I could take it back I would."

His smile was sad, his eyes sincere. He pulled all the cash from his wallet and stuck it under her coffee cup. "That's the money they paid me. Minus what I spent on gas and groceries yesterday. It doesn't make up for what I did, but I want you to have it."

"I don't want your money." She shoved the money toward him.

He shoved it back. "I don't care."

Take the damn money. The way you've been riding, you won't be winning any checks any time soon.

Huffing out a breath, she counted out the money and divided it in half and pushed his share toward him. "If you run low on cash again, you can always give rides to the next rodeo to some of the guys who don't have a vehicle. They'll pitch in for gas and usually you can pick up a few bucks cleaning stalls or doing other odd chores at the rodeo grounds. There's always someone who can use an extra hand."

"Thanks, I appreciate it."

She nodded. "Sure. Thanks for the breakfast. Again. If you want, I'll ask Josephine to have her fiancé Silas find you. He's an ex bull rider. He can get you behind the chutes. Levi's another one you should talk to, he can introduce you around."

"You two have a history."

Cora knew Ian was talking about Levi. It wasn't a question, and it wasn't something she wanted to discuss. "The man never could keep his mouth shut when he drank."

Hence the whole *poking holes in condoms* rumor. She couldn't prove he'd started it, but a good lawyer might be able to.

"It wasn't like that. Levi didn't say anything about you really. He just seemed a little protective is all."

She winced. She didn't like the reminder that she'd hurt Levi. "He wanted a relationship. I don't do them."

"Why not?"

"That's getting a little personal."

"We're friends, remember?" The smile that grew beneath the stubble on his face shouldn't have been endearing. Shouldn't have made her want more. "We even shook on it."

She couldn't—wouldn't—do this with Ian. She had her reasons, and she didn't talk about relationships any more than she had them. "I've gotta go take care of Panache, he gets grumpy when he doesn't get his grain on time."

When she went to clear the table, he stopped her. "I've got this. Thanks again for the help and the understanding. I owe you one."

A handsome man indebted to her? Yeah, she liked the sound of that. Even if they were just friends. She reached for the door knob. Over her shoulder she said, "Careful. Don't make a promise you might regret."

5

IN THE BARN LATER THAT MORNING, CORA SAT ON THE BALE OF HAY across the aisle from where Josephine stood hunched over one of Panache's front hooves, resetting the shoe he'd pulled off in his stall. She still couldn't figure out how her horse had managed that.

"Cora," Josephine said around the two horseshoe nails clamped in the corner of her mouth. "Just because Ian didn't hit on you, or try to take you to bed, means he's not interested. It doesn't mean he's gay."

Cora scoffed.

Josephine tapped in a nail and clenched it down. "Is it so unbelievable that a guy isn't into you?" Bent over the way she was, Cora couldn't see Josephine's smile, but it rang clear in her voice.

"I know there are men who aren't interested. I'm just saying that in my experience, I hadn't found many of them around here, at least not until the pregnancy scare. And—"

Josephine pulled the nails out of her mouth and glanced up. "That totally had to have been Patty Bennett who spread those rumors about the condoms."

"Patty?"

"She's sneaky, *and* she's Levi's new girl. It's no secret he's still mooning over you despite you two breaking up. What better way for Patty to make sure he doesn't come crawling back to you than to spread those lies?"

"You may have a point." Cora had always blamed the rumor on Levi, but he'd always been a decent guy. Patty made much more sense.

"Sorry," Josephine said. "I'm sure Levi and Patty are the last people you want to think about. What were you saying about guys not being interested in you?"

"That even if they aren't interested in *me*, they at least give my tits a look." Cora gave her boobs a fluff. "Ian? Nope, not so much as a glance. I mean, seriously, who could resist these?" Cora teased.

Josephine tapped in another nail. Panache swung his head around and gave the waistband of Josephine's leather chaps a tug as if telling her to hurry it up.

"Who could forget *the girls*?" Josephine looked up long enough to roll her eyes. "I mean, *I've* checked out your boobs and I'm not remotely interested. There's only one thing to do."

"What's that?"

"If you want him, ask Ian if he's gay."

Josephine finished clenching down all the nails and brought Panache's leg forward, so she could rasp the rough edges.

"I don't want him."

She stopped mid stroke and glanced over at Cora. "Seriously? He's hot. In that long, lean athletic sort of way. I've seen him jogging." Josephine waggled her brows. "I don't get the new jogging hype, but he probably has great stamina."

"Still not interested."

Josephine set Panache's hoof on the ground and leaned back against the stall, her breathing a little labored from her efforts since Panache tended to lean on Josephine whenever she lifted his leg. "Then why does it matter whether or not Ian's gay?"

She wasn't interested. Was she? After all, Ian wasn't her type, and as far away as Cora was from settling down, she knew there was a cowboy somewhere in her future, not a city slicker. Cora shrugged. "I guess it doesn't." Mostly.

Three stalls down, a door slid open and Patty Bennett came out of Levi's horse's stall, conspicuously making a point to not look in their direction.

"Speak of the devil," Josephine mumbled.

Great. "Do you think she heard?" Cora didn't know why she cared if Patty had overheard them blaming her for the rumor, considering Josephine was more than likely right. But what if she wasn't? Cora had been on the receiving end of bad talk and snide comments, and as much as she tried not to let it bother her, sometimes it did. "Maybe I should go talk to her."

Untying Panache, Josephine handed Cora the lead rope. "Let her go. I found a back paddock that's empty. We can let the horses out together and let them stretch their legs. Then it's time for you to focus. You've got your horse to take care of and your run to worry about. Right now, that's all that matters."

They bundled up against the cold and led their horses to the far back corner of the rodeo grounds and turned Comet and Panache out to run. The two horses raced up and down the fence lines, their heads high, their manes and tails flying, with white puffy clouds of condensation streaming from their noses as they snuffed and snorted. Panache skid to a stop in the corner, turned and bucked and farted and ran back down the fence line.

Cora never got tired of watching her horse run.

When the horses settled, they each found a sandy spot and collapsed in the dirt and rolled onto their backs. Then they stood, shook the dust free and started nibbling on the dead grass.

While the horses munched, Cora's mind drifted back to Ian. Was there a kernel of truth to her interest in Ian? Josephine had a point. If she didn't see Ian as anything other than a friend, why did she feel disappointed that he hadn't hit on her? She wasn't so insecure that she had to have everyone fawning over her. In fact, she preferred that they didn't...except for Ian.

Josephine leaned against the fence and tapped her boot against Cora's to get her attention. "What's the matter? Worried about the race?"

"A little." *A lot.* But the race hadn't been what she'd been thinking about. Josephine would laugh in her face if she knew that Cora had been all up in her head about Ian. The man she *wasn't* interested in. Cora said, "Don't tell Silas what I said about Ian."

Josephine pursed her lips. "I pretty much tell Silas everything. He's not like a lot of these guys. Gay or straight, Silas isn't going to care. But if it's that important to you..."

"Nah," Cora said. "I guess it's no big deal."

———

Sunday nights at the rodeo always packed in the biggest crowds. At least that's what Cora had told Ian. Apparently, everyone wanted to see who finished in the money. Then, add in the carnival crowd who'd taken over the adjacent fields, and it seemed like half the state had shown up.

Ian waited with his camera outside the uncovered warm-up arena where the barrel racers, ropers, steer wrestlers, and others warmed up their horses before competition.

Ian zipped his jacket up to his chin and pushed his new cowboy hat down farther on his head. Long ago, he'd cut the tips of the fingers off his gloves to give him more dexterity while he shot photos in the cold. He regretted that decision.

In the arena, horses and riders walked, trotted, and loped both small and large circles. A couple of the ropers had their horses on a loose rein as they twirled their ropes over their heads, their focus inward. Ian figured that like most athletes before a game, they were going through the motions in their head as well, picturing how their event would go.

"Hey, Slick," Cora's voice called out from behind him.

His heart skittered sideways, the way he'd seen a couple of the horses do when startled. Only he didn't have the excuse of being scared.

He was turned on.

The Wrangler jeans Cora had made him buy weren't going to hide that fact for long. Because the truth was, as much as he'd denied wanting to have sex with Cora, it was a damn lie.

Didn't mean he had any intention of acting on it though.

She walked toward him, her limp hardly noticeable as she led her horse. He clomped along beside her at the end of his reins. Panache was a quarter horse, that much Ian had learned already, some sort of light tan with a wide white stripe running down the length of his nose.

He'd heard the term *kind eye* tossed around here and there when people talked about horses. He looked into Panache's big brown eyes. The horse didn't look like he wanted to stomp Ian into the ground, so he figured that's what that meant.

"Slick," he said, as he ran his hand down Panache's long nose. "Very funny. I'm assuming that's short for city slicker?"

"Artistic *and* smart. Killer combo. If the rumor gets out that you have a brain, all the suitors will start flocking."

Ian glanced around. Even in his new clothes he remained practically invisible—which was fine with him—to the women. They were all drooling after the real cowboys.

Cora flipped her reins over her horse's neck, grabbed a fistful of mane, and put her left foot into the stirrup. She bounced on her right leg a couple times and cried out as she pushed off. Instead of swinging up into the saddle, she flopped over it, her belly over the seat, her right leg dangling in the air.

Panache took a couple of steps, then stopped. "A little help, here," Cora called out.

Ian slung his camera over his shoulder and hurried over and grabbed the horse's reins, even though Panache just looked at Cora over his shoulder, as if he wanted to roll his eyes.

"Not him. Me." Cora huffed and grunted.

"I don't know what to do, but I think you're embarrassing him."

"He'll get over it. Now put your hand on my ass and shove."

Okay. If she insisted. Ian palmed her fine ass and gave it a good push, allowing her to swing her leg up and over.

Josephine trotted up on her light-colored horse. A palomino, he thought Cora had called it. He'd get the lingo one of these days. Josephine gave Cora a slow clap. "The Russian judges gave you a one-point-eight for that mount."

Cora rubbed at her sore left knee and gave a mock bow while Ian pretended not to remember the feel of Cora's firm ass on his palm. The flush rushed up his face and he needlessly fiddled with his camera settings.

"Ian," Cora said, "I want you to meet Josephine's fiancé, Silas Foss."

Silas stepped around Panache and extended his hand. He had a couple of inches on Ian and some muscle. Not as much as Levi, but enough. Around his waist, Silas wore a tooled leather belt topped off with a large silver belt buckle, looking perfectly at ease in his boots and jeans and cowboy hat. Silas looked like the real deal.

Ian had looked at himself in the mirror that morning and felt like he was back in fourth grade dressing up for Halloween. How had he ever thought he could fit in? Even with the 'right' clothes, one look at him and any idiot could tell he didn't belong.

"Ian Murphy." Ian shook Silas' hand. Silas' grip was firm, but not one of those little-dick-guy shakes, where they had to prove how tough and strong they were by trying to break every bone in your hand. "Thanks for agreeing to take me behind the chutes."

"Sure thing. The bull riding is last, but we can watch the barrel races from the chutes instead of the stands if you think that might give you some better shots."

"I'll try anything once."

Ian wished the girls good luck and Josephine bent down, planting a big, fat kiss on Silas' lips. When she pulled away, Silas reached up and pulled her in for another, then whispered something in her ear. Ian averted his gaze, his eyes landing on Cora. She watched Josephine and Silas with this kinda sad, kinda happy, kinda sappy look as if she were a diabetic staring at candy she knew she couldn't have.

Cora made a face and grumbled at Ian when she caught him staring. "Don't you dare take a picture of me."

"I—" The protest sat on Ian's tongue until he glanced down at the camera in his hand, his finger already on the button. He dropped his camera, letting the strap around his neck catch it. "Sorry. Reflex."

Before Ian left, he couldn't help snapping a quick pick of the backside of Cora and Josephine riding off into the ring together, their heads tilted together, deep in conversation.

On the way to the chutes, he and Silas didn't get much of a chance to talk. It seemed like Silas knew almost everyone. He shook a lot of hands, kissed a few cheeks, and signed a couple of autographs.

Silas put a hand on Ian's shoulder and stopped him under the bleachers.

"What's up?" Ian asked.

Silas stood with his hands on his hips, looking like he had something to say but didn't know how to say it. "Um...look," he started. "These are a bunch of good guys at heart. A lot of them I'm proud to know and call my friend. They're the kind of guys that'll have your back..."

"But?"

"Sometimes they aren't tolerant of...how should I say this?" Silas thought for a second, then said, "Outsiders."

Outsiders. Would Ian always be on the outside looking in? "Nothing new to me. I get it."

"I just don't want you taking something they might say the wrong way. It's not anything they would say to your face if they got a chance to know you."

"Don't worry about me."

That seemed to mollify Silas a little, though the crease in his forehead remained. Then Silas dug the toe of his boot into the ground and kicked dirt onto Ian's boots. Ian jumped back. "Hey, man, I just bought those."

"Yeah, I know. Why do you think I'm getting them dirty? Consider it city slicker camouflage."

"Bastard," Ian teased.

Silas chuckled and clapped Ian on the shoulder. He led Ian through the chutes—a series of high metal rails designed to move cattle safely through to the arena. The bulls hadn't been brought in yet, but a few of the bull riders had made their way on back. Silas introduced Ian around. Most were friendly. A few gave him the stink eye and a reluctant handshake. One spit a wad of tobacco that splashed on Ian's boot as he walked by.

Was it the camera or was it Ian?

Silas pointed to the railings up ahead. "We can sit on top of the rails. Best view in the house."

A man approached them, giving Silas the eye that time, and flat out ignored Silas' friendly greeting. The man stomped toward Ian, his eyes narrowed, the hate rolling off him in dark, desolate waves. Ian capped his lens and fisted his hand. This probably wasn't going to end well.

The bull rider didn't take a swing at Ian, instead the guy rammed his shoulder into Ian's as he went by and muttered under his breath, "Faggot."

"Hey," Silas barked.

Ian didn't even have time to react before Silas had the man pinned against the rails, his forearm pressed against the man's throat. "Shut your damn mouth, you got me?"

The man held Silas's heated stare for a beat or two, then shoved Silas away, disappearing down the chutes without a backward glance.

Ian looked around, most of the men hadn't noticed. A few had but quickly glanced away.

"I can see why you like these guys so much." Ian layered on the sarcasm the same way he'd layered grease on an old axel back at his father's garage, extra thick.

"Sorry about that. I warned you some of them were intolerant assholes."

Ian didn't really understand the animosity some of the riders had for him, but he didn't let it get to him. Maybe they'd had bad experiences with photographers or outsiders in the past.

Either way, a rough day behind the chutes topped any day back home. "You did, and while I appreciate you sticking up for me, I'm perfectly capable of taking care of myself."

Silas grinned. "That's what Levi said." Then his smile faded, and he added, "But seriously, you shouldn't have to put up with that shit just because you're gay."

Ian barked out a laugh. "You think I'm gay?"

"It's okay, man." Silas clapped him on the upper arm. "I have an uncle who's gay. I don't give a flying fig who you fuck."

Silas climbed up the rails and Ian scrambled up after him.

They settled on top, hooking their heels on one of the rails below to keep from falling off.

"I would say your secret is safe with me," Silas said, "but clearly the word already got around."

Ian laughed again. "Not that I think there's anything wrong with being gay. I mean, it's the seventies. Free love and all that. But, I'm not gay. I don't know where you heard it, but you're wrong."

Silas cursed under his breath as understanding sank in. "Buddy, I think I know two women who owe you an apology."

———

CORA HEARD THE SNAP OF IAN'S SHUTTER BEFORE SHE HEARD THE scuff of his boots in the barn aisle. Up and down the barn, people were busy taking care of their horses, getting them fed and watered and settled in for the night. Josephine had already finished up, but it wouldn't be long until Cora would be nearly alone.

The barns late at night were one of her favorite places. A place where she could sit in the quiet with her thoughts, with nothing but the smells of fresh hay and manure, the rhythmic munching of feed, the soft nickers, the occasional rapid-fire *bam, bam*, as a disgruntled horse kicked at its stall.

Panache stood beside her in the aisle, nibbling on the hay bale she was currently using as a seat. She scrunched her fingers through Panache's forelock.

She *belonged* here.

But unless she started winning, she'd have to quit and find a job. The bull and bronc riders had it easier when it came to expenses. At least they didn't have an extra mouth to feed, not to mention the stall fees, and God forbid, vet bills.

Cora glanced over at Ian as he took one last photo and

reloaded his camera. She patted the end of the hay bale. "Have a seat. Did you get some good pictures tonight?"

"A few, I think. We'll see once I get the negatives developed."

When he sat, Panache gave him a quick sniff but went back to the hay when Ian didn't cough up a treat. Ian wiggled his camera. "You don't have to worry, I'm not selling those shots of you. I hate wasting film and I needed to finish up that roll. I'll give you the negatives and everything."

At that point, having her picture in the paper again was the least of her worries. "'S'okay. In fact, I should be thanking you. If it hadn't been for the money you gave me, I'd already be broke."

"That was a tough break tonight," he said. "At least you didn't knock down any barrels."

Cora twirled her hand in the air, an unenthusiastic 'whoo hoo.' "A three-legged pony could have run that race faster."

"Not true. The two of you were flying. You were only out of the money by one one-hundredth of a second."

"Might as well have been a minute. At least Josephine finished in the money, so we can afford the gas to Albuquerque tomorrow."

He replaced the cap on his camera and placed it in his upturned cowboy hat and set it beside him. He rubbed his hands up and down his thighs. "Uh...if you want, you can save your money and ride with me to Albuquerque. Josephine can give someone else a ride to split the gas money."

She glanced up at him, surprised by his generosity. He'd already given her money. Ian wasn't exactly loaded down with cash himself. "Why would you do that?"

"It's a long, boring drive to Albuquerque. I wouldn't mind the company."

Her stomach fluttered, and for a second there she thought she recognized a spark of interest in his eyes. She should do what Josephine suggested and flat out ask him if he was gay.

But then he said, "You know, as friends."

As if she didn't need him to make that any more abundantly clear.

"Besides, I still feel bad about selling that photo to the papers. If I can help you out, I want to."

It should have made her feel good that he wanted to help her, but if he'd only offered to assuage his guilt, then she wanted nothing to do with it. She didn't want Ian's pity, or anyone else's. "Thanks, but Josephine and I are travel partners. I'd hate to leave her to deal with the horses by herself."

Which was a complete lie. There had been numerous times when Josephine had taken the horses while Cora rode with some other cowboy, or Cora drove while Josephine had ridden with Silas. Sure, they traveled together, but they weren't exactly attached at the hip either. It all had evened out in the end.

Ian shrugged. "Suit yourself. Offer stands if you change your mind."

Cora pulled her knees to her chest and settled her arms around her legs. "Thanks."

They lapsed into silence. It wasn't exactly awkward, so Cora didn't bother with any small talk. She wasn't in the mood anyway.

"So, are you going to sit here all night and mope?"

That pulled a huff of a laugh out of her. She looked over at him. He had the sexy asshole smirk down cold.

"I was thinking about it." Then her stomach grumbled and growled, sounding as if she'd swallowed a couple of pissed off pumas.

"Maybe you should think about getting something to eat."

"I had a PB&J at noon."

Ian glanced at his watch. "That was more than ten hours ago. You didn't have any dinner?"

Cora shrugged, and the heat crept into her cheeks. At least

the lighting was bad enough to probably hide her embarrass-ment. "Like I said. Limited funds." She patted the hay bale. "I'm on my last bale of hay and I'm near the bottom of a bag of feed. I don't have money to blow."

"You can't go all day without eating."

"I do what I have to do. Besides, Panache is the one who has to run. I just have to hang on."

"I saw you women race tonight. You do a hell of a lot more than hang on."

Just because Ian was right, didn't negate the fact she had to cut corners to save money, and if she had to cut corners, her horse wasn't going to suffer for it. Her stomach growled again as the pumas started an all-out brawl.

"Jesus Christ." Ian took Panache's rope from her hands and stood. "I've got a better idea. Go to the carnival with me. We can blow off some steam and I'll buy you a beer and a hot dog."

"I have bread and peanut butter back at the trailer. I don't need your pity."

He scrubbed a hand down his face. "Good Lord. Are all you Texas women so stubborn?"

By all accounts, Ian hadn't even tried hiding his exaspera-tion. He also didn't give her a chance to answer. "It's not pity. It's what friends do."

Friends. Yeah. How could she forget?

6

THE CARNIVAL WAS IN FULL SWING BY THE TIME IAN PAID THEIR entry and bought a string of tickets for rides and games. Multi-color lights flashed, kids screamed, couples laughed, and teens stole kisses in the dark.

To his credit, he only stopped one time to take a picture on the way to the food stands. Of all the pictures he'd taken that night, excluding the photos he'd taken of Cora and Panache in the barn, developing that picture excited him the most. In the foreground, he'd framed a crying kid, with an empty cone and a blob of ice cream in the dirt, in mid-field, a man handing his girlfriend a prize, and in the background the Ferris wheel, with the silhouette of two teens kissing at the top.

Everything a carnival should be in one picture.

"Sorry," he said as he straightened and capped his lens.

Cora cocked her head and smiled at him as if something inside her brain had clicked into place. "You really can't help yourself, can you?"

"No. I'd say it was in my blood, but I'm the only photographer in the family. My mother gave me my first camera for my birthday when I was only eight. My Da about lost his shit. Said we didn't have the money to blow like that, but my mother refused to take it back."

They took their spot at the back of the food line to wait their turn. "You've stuck with photography ever since?"

"I did, mostly. For a kid, film was expensive, and no way would my dad spend any money on it. I did odd jobs like sweeping sidewalks to buy my own film. I even taught myself how to develop it to save money. By not having money to waste, it also made me more careful of my shots. In my mind, every shot had to count."

"So, you knew from the start you were destined to do this as a career?"

"Not even." The people in front of them got their food and moved out of the way. Ian and Cora placed their orders. "I didn't look at it as anything other than a hobby, until a picture in a magazine changed my view of the world."

Cora tossed him a skeptical look. "One picture changed your whole world view?"

"One picture." Ian took their food and thanked the attendant. Cora grabbed the beers and they weaved their way through the picnic tables until they found an empty one. They set their food and drinks down, and Cora tossed a couple of empty cups that had been left behind into a nearby garbage can.

Not wasting any time, Cora squirted on the ketchup and stuffed the end of the hot dog into her mouth. She'd worked her way through about a third of it when she washed the bite down with a swig of beer and said, "Someday, I'd like to see a picture that powerful."

Ian froze, the cup of beer at his lips. He set the cup down. "You're not just saying that, are you?"

"Of course not."

Ian reached for his wallet, hesitated, then figured, what the fuck. He'd never told anyone about the photo, much less ever shown it to anyone. Not because it was a deep, dark secret, but because no one had been interested enough to ever ask.

Carefully, he withdrew the tattered magazine clipping from his wallet, unfolded it and held it out to her. She wiped her fingers and took it. He didn't move around the table to look at it over her shoulder.

Over the years, he'd stared at that photo for hours and hours and still it had a visceral power over him. Much more than a gut check. More of a stripping of your heart from your chest, and your soul from your body, leaving you bleeding and raw and full of despair.

Cora gasped. "That poor boy...are...are those..."

Even today, all these years later, Ian had to clear his throat. "His parents. A tiny village in North Korea." Ian knew the name of the village, but the name didn't matter. In his mind, he saw the crumbling wall behind the blindfolded, knobby kneed boy with three rifles aimed at his head. The boy couldn't have been any older than eight. The same age Ian had been when he'd received his first camera.

Maybe that's why he'd identified with it so much. While his father and his brothers had picked on him, at least he had a roof over his head, food in his belly, shoes on his feet, and clothes that weren't tattered and torn.

And no rifles aimed at his head.

"What happened?" Cora's words sounded hollow as if the picture had drained her. He knew the feeling.

"The boy's father had spoken out against the government, the story said. The family paid the price of their defiance with their lives, including the boy."

"The boy..." Cora ran her finger down the stoic figure. "He has to know what's happening, but he's standing tall, his fists clenched, as if unwilling to give the soldiers the satisfaction of breaking him." Cora handed the photo back to Ian, swiping moisture from her cheek. "It's very powerful. I can see where it would have affected you."

Ian carefully folded and replaced the article in his wallet. "It's more than just what the picture represented. It was also the first time I realized that you could make a living with photography and that the work could matter. That you could impact other people's lives as well as the whole world.

"I've followed the photographer's, Edward Lark's, career ever since. Kind of my mentor from afar. He used to work for the *New York Times* before he became a freelancer and traveled the world in search of stories. It's one of the reasons why I want to win the magazine contest and the assignment. The winner will be paired with him for a time. It would be my chance to change the world, even if it is only one person at a time, the way Lark's photograph did for me."

He ducked his head as the heat climbed up his cheeks. Talk about running off at the mouth. He—

Ian got bumped from behind, and a cup full of ice landed in his face. Before he could even react, a man said, "We don't like your kind around here."

Ian thought about going after the guy, but this was a family place. He wasn't going to get into a fight here. Not over something as insignificant as ice in the face. But Cora jumped up and he had to grab her arm and sit her back down.

"Let it go," Ian said. "He's not worth our time."

"Are you kidding me?" Cora's voice rose and the people who didn't know anything had happened, now stared. "That asshole threw ice in your face. What did he mean about not liking your kind around here? Who was that?"

Ian grabbed a couple of the napkins off the table and dried off. "I have no idea."

As much as he wanted the satisfaction of punching the smirk off the jackass's face, doing so wouldn't make the guy any less of a bigot. Besides, they were here to cheer Cora up, not get arrested for assault and battery.

"*Ian*," Cora leaned forward, keeping her voice down so she wouldn't draw any more attention. "What's going on?"

He'd had every intention of talking to Cora about the rumor, but he hadn't wanted to do it that night when she was already feeling bad. Unfortunately, one look at Cora's face and he knew she wasn't about to let it drop.

"There's a rumor going around that I'm gay," Ian said.

Cora's hands flew to her mouth, covering her gasp. "That wasn't...I didn't...I...I'm so sorry, Ian."

After what Silas had said, Ian already suspected the rumor had originated with Cora. His chest pinched. It hurt more than it should, having his suspicions confirmed. "Silas figured you girls owed me an apology. I guess he was right."

"What does Silas have to do with this?"

Ian told her about the encounters behind the chutes, and about what Silas had determined based on what Josephine told him. Ian had still held out hope that Silas had been wrong.

Cora picked at her hot dog bun, the meat now long cold. "Why didn't you say anything to me earlier?"

"What am I going to say? 'Mommy, someone called me names and hurt my feelings?'"

Cora hid her face in her hands then peeked out from between her fingers. "You still should have said something to me. In my defense, it's not like I went around the rodeo telling everyone you were gay. Josephine and I were talking about it and I think Patty Bennett must have overheard. It wouldn't be the first rumor she started. Besides, what business is it of anybody's if you're gay?"

"Cora," he said. It took a few seconds for her to look at him. When he had her attention, he continued, "I'm not into men."

"Shit." She thumped her forehead on the picnic table. "That

only makes it worse. Or does that make it better? I don't even know anymore." Her face fell, and her eyes glistened in the twinkling carnival lights. "I really am sorry, Ian."

"Forget about it. It'll all blow over in a few days." In all honesty, he was more put out that she hadn't finished her food. She needed to eat. He pointed to her hot dog. "Want me to buy you a hot one?"

She took a bite, tucked it into her cheek and said, "It's fine. Don't waste your money."

When they'd finished, they walked the concourse, but Ian couldn't reconcile why Cora had thought he wasn't into women. "I don't understand why you thought I was gay."

"This is going to sound so stupid and self-centered." Cora folded and refolded the string of tickets in her hand. She didn't look at him when she said, "You never hit on me. You never tried to sneak a look when I changed clothes. Even when I was drunk, when you took me back to your place and had me in your bed, you didn't make any lewd remarks or sly innuendos. Or slip in next to me in the middle of the night. *Nothing*."

She stopped in the middle of a throng of people and looked at him. "Do you know how many times that has happened to me since I've hit puberty?"

The sea of people parted around them. Cora's question seemed mostly rhetorical, but he said, "I'm gonna guess, not many."

He took her elbow and guided her along, so they wouldn't block traffic and piss anyone else off. He'd had enough of that for one day.

"You'd be correct. I told Josephine my suspicions, more as a joke than anything serious. I thought we were alone, but Patty was three stalls down and apparently she overheard, and Patty's the last person you ever want to tell a secret to and, and, and...really, what was I supposed to think?" her voice ran the range from soft and apologetic to shrill and incredulous.

Ian guided them toward the games. They passed the shooting gallery and a dunk tank, the carnies talking it up, trying to part them from their money. "Maybe you were supposed to think that I don't bed women when they're drunk, that—"

She gave him a playful whack on the arm. "I wasn't *that* drunk."

He leaned in and said, "Sweetheart, I don't know how things work in your little world, but in my world when a man doesn't take advantage of a woman when she's vulnerable, that makes him a gentleman, *not* gay."

She stepped back. "Now you're pissed."

The more he thought about it, the angrier he got until he wasn't sure why he tried to hide how he felt. What kind of men had she been dating that that kind of behavior had become the norm for her?

"I'm beyond pissed and have moved to furious." Heat infused his cheeks and he felt that vessel thump at his temple. "Why would you put up with men who treated you that way? Why—"

"Wait. You're not mad I thought you were gay. You're mad about the way other men have treated me."

"*Yes.*" He wanted to ring a bell and give her the biggest stuffed animal at the fair. "The gay thing will blow over. It's the way you expect men to treat you is what needs to change. You deserve much better than that."

Cora stood and stared at him as if she were looking at something she'd never seen before. Finally, she said, "You're right." Her voice cracked, and Ian had to lean in to hear her over the hoots and hollers of the crowd. "I've always expected the worst behavior from men because that's what I've always known." She raised up on her tiptoes and pressed a chaste kiss to his cheek.

"You're a good man, Ian Murphy. I should never have underestimated you."

————

TWO WEEKS, ANOTHER THOUSAND MILES AND SEVERAL POOR RUNS later, the light knock came on Cora's trailer door at oh-god-it's-too-early. Cora groaned and cracked open an eye. From her vantage point on the top bunk of Josephine's trailer, she could see straight out the narrow front window. It was still dark.

Ian knocked again. She knew it was Ian because in a moment of sheer stupidity, she'd asked him to take her with him on one of his pre-dawn photo shoots, wanting to see more of the world through his eyes. The worst part? She couldn't even claim she'd been drunk at the time.

"I know you're in there," Ian called out. "This was your idea, not mine."

"For the love of Pete, let the man in." Josephine's whine came out muffled, her head still under the covers.

"Coming," Cora said as she swung down from her bunk.

She dressed in record time, for once foregoing full makeup. Anyone who woke her this early, deserved what they got. She flipped the switch on the door lock and stuck her head out. The air was mild and muggy for a mid-November day but that's what she loved about the Corpus Christi fairgrounds in the winter. "Almost ready."

Ian turned toward her and awkwardly dug his hands into his pockets, as if he didn't know what to do with his hands without his camera in them.

Cora stepped out of the trailer in her sock feet, carrying her boots and a hair tie. "Um...is there a reason you're staring at me?" He really was cute when he was flustered. "Never seen a woman without makeup before?"

"Women, yes. You? No." He glanced away, but as she slipped on her boots and tamed her unruly morning hair into a ponytail, his gaze kept returning to her.

Maybe she should have rethought that whole going without makeup thing. She'd have felt less exposed if she'd come out in her underwear. "Can you give me a sec? I just want to put on a little mascara and blush...and maybe a swipe or two of lipstick."

Ian grabbed her by the arm before she could retreat inside. "You don't have time. We're going to miss the best light if we don't leave now."

In the end she got him to concede to a quick trip to the restroom, so she could pee and brush her teeth, but he'd been tapping his foot outside the women's restroom the whole time. When she got out, she snagged the Mets baseball cap from his head and plopped it on hers.

He snatched it back, but instead of putting it on his head, he flipped the bill around backward and plunked it back down on hers. "That's better."

She preferred the bill in front. A little camouflage for her face at least. "Why'd you do that?"

"You have a beautiful face, Cora. I don't understand why you'd want to hide it behind a layer of makeup or the bill of a cap."

Her eyes met his, waiting for the punchline. There wasn't one. Or maybe that was Ian's way of hitting on her. Her face must have looked suspicious because he quickly added, "That's a compliment, not a come-on."

Of course, it wasn't. Which stung. She tried to ignore it. After all, they were just *friends*, right? "Yeah. Okay." She waved a hand in his general direction to get the focus off her. "Aren't you forgetting something?"

Ian started back across the parking lot and she fell into step beside him as a streak of lighter gray appeared on the horizon. "The camera's already in the truck."

Truck? "Where are we going?"

"Can't get this close to the beach and not take photos of the Gulf Coast at sunrise."

They climbed into his truck and made the short drive to the beach. They pulled into a parking lot next to a filled-to-capacity RV park that catered to the snowbirds. But even with all the winter tourists, at that early hour, they had the beach to themselves.

Ian retrieved his Nikon, equipped with his wide-angle lens and slung his camera bag over his shoulder. Obviously, she'd been spending way too much time with him if she could recognize his different lenses on sight. Considering how her runs had gone lately, maybe she needed to concentrate more on her riding and less on a certain photographer.

She picked up his tripod. They'd only made it a short way up the beach before they shucked their boots and socks and rolled their pants up to their knees. The light breeze rolled the waves to shore in lazy, gentle sheets. Shorebirds pecked at the sand in the shallows, while a pair of pelicans glided by, the tips of their wings skimming the smooth surface of the water.

Cora splashed around in the ankle-deep water while Ian set up his camera and tripod. The low light made the water sparkle and shine as if someone had tossed their hand in the air and scattered diamonds across the vast horizon.

When he finished with his sunrise shots, she tagged along as he made his way up the beach, the fine grains of sand sticking to her toes and the bottoms of her feet. He didn't waste his film on the requisite long shots down the shoreline, but instead he concentrated on the little things. Both the good and the bad.

The play of light and shadow across water-rippled sand, the ghost crab as it carried breakfast back into its tunnel, the scramble of a late hatching turtle as it scurried into the surf, the battered body of a dead pelican pushed to shore with a tangle of plastic from a six-pack wrapped around its neck.

She turned away and bent to pick up a shell in the shallows that had caught her eye. The shutter on Ian's camera click, click, clicked, and Cora glanced up expecting to see fish jumping or dolphins swimming in the shallows, but Ian's camera wasn't pointing toward the ocean, he had the lens aimed at her.

"I thought you didn't like wasting your film," Cora said, oddly pleased to find his attention back on her. "You'll never win the contest that way."

He lowered the lens. "As much as I want to win, sometimes it's the journey that's most important, not the destination. I'm trying not to lose sight of that along the way."

Capping his lens, he packed up his gear and shouldered his bag. "Besides, I'm going to need something to remember you by when I'm famous and living halfway across the world."

Right. Temporary gig.

In a short time, she'd come to take his being there for granted. Like him cooking her breakfast in the morning if she made it over to his trailer after his morning shoots.

That he'd be there in the alley when she and Panache galloped by after one of her runs.

That he'd meet her at her stall after the rodeo with a beer and a helping hand.

That they'd hang out at his trailer until all hours of the night as he developed his best photos of the day.

She waggled her fingers for his camera. "My turn."

For a second, she thought he wouldn't give it up, then a slow smile spread across his face. "This should be interesting."

She brought the viewer to her eye and twisted him into focus, liking the way the sun glinted off the red highlights in his dark stubble, how the life shined in his eyes, how his amusement turned his lips just so. She pressed the shutter and in that flash of a moment, he stuck his tongue out at her.

"Hey! You messed up my shot. Now I've only got one left."

"No one wants to see pictures of me."

"I do." The honest response was out before she had a chance to sensor it. Then she decided she wouldn't have censored her words if she could, because unless the people judging the contest were blind idiots, he would be leaving, and taking his friendship with him.

It's not just his friendship you will miss.

Okay. She'd miss him, too. There wasn't any shame in admitting that. When she went to take his picture again, he covered the lens with his hand. "Seriously," he said.

The light dimmed in his eyes. She couldn't tell if it was from a demon from his past or the cloud passing in front of the sun.

"Don't tell me the photographer is camera shy."

"I just prefer being behind the lens." His tone came out even, but unnaturally so, as if he had to work at it to make it sound normal.

"Why do I get the feeling there's a story there?"

He scrubbed his hand over the back of his neck before finally meeting her gaze. "My mother took a picture of me right before she died. Before I knew the world could be such a dark place. I still have the negative, but I haven't been able to bring myself to print it yet."

"I'm so sor—" she started to apologize, but he cut her off with a wave of his hand.

"It's silly really." He had to clear his throat to continue. "It was a long time ago."

For an inexplicable reason it became important to have a picture of him. If he was going to disappear from her life, she needed something to remember the man who was slowly making her see a world beyond barrel racing and rodeos and nights on the town and remember the friendship that was coming to mean so much to her.

She lowered the camera. "Will you take one with me?"

With his hands on his hips, he stared at the ground before answering. "Don't you have a horse to feed?"

"Panache always thinks he's starving. I'm pretty sure two minutes one way or the other isn't going to kill him."

Just when Cora was convinced he'd say no, he said, "Sure, why not?" His words lacked any real enthusiasm, but she'd take what she could get.

Using the tripod, Ian got the camera ready, set the timer, then dashed back around in front of the lens. He put his arm around her waist and she turned toward him and draped her hands on his shoulder and smiled at the camera.

The light on the body of the camera blinked faster and at the last second, she turned toward him and planted a kiss on his cheek.

7

———

"I'm sorry I kissed you," Cora said, breaking the awkward silence as Ian drove them back to the rodeo grounds. "I didn't mean anything by it. I know you're not interested."

"It's not that." The words were out before he could stop them. She stilled beside him. When would he learn to keep his mouth shut? He didn't want to give her any false hope that they could ever be anything other than friends. Even if at times he'd wished for more.

She plucked his hat off her head. "If this is the *it's not you it's me* speech, don't bother."

They had their windows down, the mild winter wind buffeting the interior and whipping the wisps of hair that had come free of her ponytail.

"It's the *timing is bad, I wish things were different, but they're not*, speech."

"Yeah, because that's so much better."

Cora fiddled with the brim of his cap. It had the perfect curve to it that he'd perfected over years of wear, and she unwittingly mangled it.

But her wear and tear on his heart? Even more damaging

80

and not as easy to fix. Why did he always want what he couldn't have?

He turned into the parking lot of the rodeo grounds and headed around to the backside of the arena where all the trailers were parked. "Look, my focus is on my career, and I don't like starting things I can't finish. We agreed to be just friends. I think it's best if our relationship stays that way."

Yeah, just keep telling yourself that buddy. Is that why you've been running around all morning with a semi hard-on in your pants? Because you think it's best if you two stayed friends?

Stupid thing was, he'd only gotten harder since that kiss, thanks to his dick's overactive imagination. He could have understood his body's reaction if she'd shoved her tongue down his throat and they did the tonsil tango. But all it had been was a chaste peck on the cheek.

"Oh shit." Something in Cora's voice made him glance over at her. The color had leached from her face and her hand gripped the door latch. For a second, he feared she'd throw herself out of the rolling truck.

He slowed and followed her gaze. At the door of her trailer stood a thin man with a clean-shaven face, a shock of gray hair, and a clerical collar around his neck.

By the scowl on the man's face, and the way he pounded on the door of the trailer with the meat of his fist, Ian knew that if he walked in on the man's sermons it would be all fire and brimstone, hell and wrath, devil and doom, not peace and love and forgiveness.

"Stop," Cora said. "Stop right here."

Ian stomped on the brakes and the truck lurched to a stop. Ian stared out the windshield. The man's gaze brushed past Ian's truck. "Who is it?"

"I-It's my father."

He waited a beat, then two as that declaration sank in.

"Park over there." Cora pointed over to their right where an outbuilding would block his truck from view.

He did what she asked, then cut the engine. They sat in near silence, the rasp of her breath the only sound. With exaggerated care, she laid his hat on the seat between them and dried her hands on the legs of her jeans.

Clearly, she didn't want to be seen driving up with him, but when she popped her door latch, Ian reached for his. No way he'd let her face her father without him there. Especially since he had a good suspicion the man had shown up at her trailer because of him and that damn picture of her he'd sold to the *El Paso Tribune*.

"Don't," she said as he went to get out of his truck. "If he sees you, it will only make it worse. Trust me on this. I need to do this alone."

"I should be there. It's my fault. I can expl—"

She placed her hand on his. "You had no way of knowing. This isn't your fault. This has been a long time coming. The photo just gave him an excuse to come now."

"I'm responsible. This is my mess. I should clean it up."

"No. This is on me. You didn't pour those drinks down my throat or lift me on top of those tables. It wasn't the first time."

Then she got this smile, an intoxicating mix of sass and devil-may-care that almost had him reaching for her and pulling her in for a real kiss. Which wouldn't solve anything. Especially not the riot in his head nor the hard-on in his pants.

"If truth be told," she said, "it probably won't be the last time either."

She slid out of his truck as he drummed his fingers on the steering wheel. Had she really expected him to sit there and let her take all the heat?

Ian slipped out of the truck and shouldered his camera bag, closing the door quietly behind him. He had to respect that she didn't want him there when she confronted her father, but that didn't mean he wouldn't be there for her if she needed him.

From the back side of the outbuilding, he cut his way under the bleacher stands and came out near some of the chutes that fed into the arena. This time of day, the chutes were empty of animals and most people. Ian set his tripod up with his tele-photo lens and aimed it at Cora and her father. With most of his body behind a support column, Ian wouldn't be visible from this distance unless someone looked carefully.

Besides, it couldn't really be called eavesdropping when the voices didn't carry the distance. Could it?

Through his viewfinder, Ian watched Cora. She'd stopped behind one of the dumpsters, bent over, hands on her knees. He almost dropped everything and went to her, but then she straightened and approached her father. Her steps faltered at first, then as she got closer, her shoulders went back, her chin went up, and she strode forward with grace and purpose. That's his girl.

His girl?

Not hardly.

But if things were different...

"Hey, Murph," Smokey Dunn, one of the team ropers who had given him a hard time called out from behind him, using the shortened version of his last name as if they were friends. For the record, when someone tried to beat the gay out of you, you were *not* friends.

Ian's heart kicked in his chest, not from fear, but from antici-pation. He'd like to take that asshole on, man to man, without a group of his buddies to back him up, and see how well Dunn fared. News flash...it would be a hell of a lot worse than the last time.

Ian turned to face Dunn. "What do you want?"

Instead of the sneer Ian had come to expect from the roper,

the man had a sheepish smile. Dunn removed his cowboy hat and wiped the sweat from his brow before replacing it, a nervous gesture since it wasn't particularly warm out, especially there under the stands.

"I came to offer you an apology," Dunn said, his hand outstretched.

Ian ignored the proffered hand. Even though he didn't need the bigot's apology, and he wanted to turn his focus back to Cora and her father, Ian found himself saying, "For what? The name calling? The shoving? The kidney punch?"

Dunn dropped his hand. "All of it. Look, man, me and the boys...we were assholes. Simple as that. You're an all right guy."

"Why the change of heart?"

"A couple of Silas's buddies set us right. We didn't know you was really straight."

"I don't know if it bothers me more that you and your goons hated me because you thought I was gay, or that you think I'm all right now that the news has started to get around that I'm straight. You are a perfect example that a man's character isn't determined by where he puts his dick."

Dunn had the decency to look chagrined. He glanced away, then back again. "So, we good?"

They were a long way from good, but Ian had more important things to worry about other than Dunn's homophobia. "Sure."

Dunn tipped his hat and walked away. Ian returned his attention to Cora at the opposite end of his lens. He twisted her into better focus, zooming in on her face, on the hot mix of emotions.

More than simple anger. Her expression ran the gamut from fear, disappointment, regret, determination, steadfastness, all tumbled together with a child's unfailing need for their parents' approval. He recognized it because he'd seen that need staring back at him in the mirror more times than he'd like to admit.

His shutter clicked before he'd even realized he'd reached for the shutter release button. Then in a blur, she disappeared from the frame. Ian stood and watched as her father dragged her toward a boat-sized metallic-red Cadillac. New and shiny. A seventy-two or seventy-three model. Her father tore open the passenger door. Cora kicked it closed and wrenched her arm free.

Ian had closed half the distance between him and the car before he'd realized he'd made the decision to help. Their raised voices carried over the chug of a tractor as it brought a bucket full of dirty shavings out of the barn.

"I'm not going home, Father," Cora said. "This is my life. This is where I belong."

"I will not have my daughter make a fool out of me and her mother. You are the laughing stock of the whole congregation. How can I be expected to be a shepherd for my people when I can't even control my own daughter?"

Cora laughed, but disgust beat out any humor. "Your congregation. All my life I've had to live up to not only your expectations, but the congregation's as well. No one can measure up to that, no matter how perfect they are."

"You never even tried."

"I tried. God knows, I tried."

Her father reopened the passenger door. "Get in. I'm not asking again."

Cora's gaze shifted from the car to her father and back again. Was she seriously contemplating going with him? What about her barrel racing? Her horse. Her friends. *Him?*

So, it's okay for you to leave her, but not okay for her to leave you? Is that it?

Ian refused to answer that. All he knew was he couldn't let

her get in that car. He increased his pace, almost breaking into a run. That's when she glanced up and saw him coming. She shook her head. Was that for him or her father?

Ian slowed. Stopped.

Cora took a step back and asked her father, "Is that a promise?"

Her father closed the distance between them. "*Cora.*"

Cora's face started to fall as she slowly backed away. "Good-bye, Father. Tell Mom I love her."

Then she turned and ran toward the barn. Ian followed, grabbing up his gear along the way. She may not want to see him, but he wanted her to know he was there if she needed him.

———

PANACHE MUNCHED AWAY ON HIS PELLETS AND CORA SHOVED MORE hay into his hay bag, as the tears of anger and frustration and futility ran down her cheeks. She swiped at them with the heels of her hands, her anger growing with each tear shed.

That her father's disappointment in her could still affect her like that, after all these years, only made her feel worse. She was an adult. She could live her life the way she wanted, she didn't need his approval or blessing.

Grabbing the manure fork and wheel barrow, she started cleaning Panache's stall, concentrating on the burn in the muscles of her arms, shoulders, and back as she shoveled soiled shavings. The manure landed in the metal wheel barrow with soft thuds.

The slow, steady munching of hay, and the nickers of horses in nearby stalls as their owners brought them feed and hay soothed her emotional jagged edges. This argument with her father wasn't anything new, but that didn't make it hurt any less.

She caught movement out of the corner of her eye, and even

before she glanced up, she knew who stood by the stall door. Ian. He leaned against the stall entrance, one foot crossed over the other. With his long, lean, athletic body, Ian looked good in boots and Wranglers. He'd rolled the sleeves of his blue western shirt up his forearms. The only thing missing was his cowboy hat.

A zing of awareness heated her chest and skipped along her nerves until her fingertips and girly bits buzzed. She seriously needed to rethink her I-only-date-cowboys rule.

"You okay?" he asked.

Leaning on her manure fork she said, "Would you believe me if I said yes?"

"Nope."

She went back to the stall cleaning, working extra hard on the stubborn pee spot in the middle. "How much did you hear."

"Enough." Taking the manure fork and setting it aside, Ian rolled the wheel barrow into the aisle. "Enough to know your father is an absolute ass. Enough to know you didn't deserve anything he dished out."

Panache left his feed long enough to suck down half of the water in his bucket. If her horse missed her crying in his mane, he didn't say. If truth be told, Panache probably appreciated having Ian as backup. She suspected her emotional, roller coaster life might be more than one horse could handle.

"It's nothing new. In fact, my father should probably thank me. I can't tell you the number of sermons I've inspired over the years. All the sideways glances from the congregation during services made it perfectly clear they knew where he'd gotten his ideas."

"He had no right to drag your mistakes out in front of all your friends and neighbors and make you his ceremonial whipping girl."

At the time, she hadn't seen it that way. It had just been her life. Though living under her town's microscope had made her twitchy the older she got. The scrutiny should have made her watch her step, but Cora wasn't wired that way. If nothing else, she'd been a cautionary tale for the town's kids.

Still, that didn't explain why her heart sat so heavy in her chest, or why her eyes stung with tears that threatened to fall again. She wasn't naive enough to think her parents would agree with everything she'd ever done, but of all the things her parents had taught her, the right from wrong, the good from evil, the sinner from the saint, the lesson that had stuck with her the most had become the truest of them all...love was conditional.

"Damn it." She swiped at her cheeks. Stupid tears.

"Oh, baby." The soft, soothing way his words came out felt like a balm on her chaffed emotions. He took her face in his hands and smoothed away the wetness with his thumbs. "Nobody deserves to be treated like that. Especially a heart as sweet and genuine as yours."

Despite all her efforts, a sob escaped, and Ian gathered her in his arms and held her tight through the worst of the crying. He soothed her with words that she felt more than heard, his hands gentle as they stroked her hair and held her head to his chest, his heart beating strong and steady and true.

By the time she'd finished blubbering, his shirt was damp, and her temples throbbed with the beginnings of a headache. She needed to get her mind off her father. "Tell me about your family."

He chuckled, and shifted her in his arms, but he didn't let her go. She was okay with that. "If you're looking for a happy story, you've picked the wrong shoulder to cry on."

She pulled back enough to see his face, her hand coming to rest on his chest. "It doesn't have to be happy, just real."

Swallowing hard, Ian said, "Real?...Fuck...All right. My whole life my father and brothers treated me as if I didn't belong. That I wasn't one of them. That I wasn't a real Murphy."

Ian paused, his focus going inward. Cora waited him out, not wanting to interrupt. "You see my father and brothers all have red hair and are fair skinned, but I'm what you call a black Irish. My mother had darker hair. I didn't think anything about it. Mostly. Until..."

His voice faded out and he went quiet for so long she feared he wouldn't continue. But somehow knowing his childhood hadn't been perfect either made her feel not quite so alone in the world. She should have told him it was okay, that he didn't have to tell her anything he didn't want to, but a small part of her needed to hear it. It was that part of her that waited through the silence.

Ian cleared his throat. "Until a few days before I left the Bronx." Glancing down, Ian met her gaze for the first time since he started his story. "That's when I found out that my father wasn't really my father."

"Oh, no." Cora's chest tightened as if one the ropers had used her for a practice dummy. "I'm sorry."

"I'm not." Ian's conviction made Cora believe him. "It explains so much. The truth is, the more I think about it, the more I'm glad to know I'm not Patrick Murphy's spawn.

"Spawn. You make it sound like your siblings are the seeds of the devil."

"If the truth fits." Ian laughed it off as if his brothers weren't *that* bad.

"Do you know who your real father is?"

"No clue."

"Maybe he was a photographer too. Maybe it's in your blood. Maybe that's why your mother gave you the camera for your birthday."

"Could be."

"Are you going to look for him?"

"Naw." Ian shook his head, though the way he hesitated before he did made Cora think that he harbored some curiosity about his real father. "I wouldn't even begin to know where to start. Besides, I'm not a kid that needs his daddy."

"No, you're not a kid. But that doesn't mean you don't need him, that having him in your life couldn't be a positive thing."

"Ha. Yeah. I don't think I need a man in my life who refused to claim his son."

She could understand his bitterness, the sense of rejection he must feel. Briefly, she wondered if it would hurt more to be rejected by the father you knew or know that your father couldn't even be bothered to get to know you before rejecting you. But everything in life wasn't black or white.

"Maybe it wasn't like that. Maybe he doesn't even know he's a father," she said.

Ian shifted and let his head fall back against the stall, staring off into the distance. He took in a deep breath and blew it out. "I hadn't thought about it that way. Wrapping my head around my mother's infidelity has been difficult enough. Though honestly, I can't blame her for it. Patrick Murphy isn't a lovable man."

"I could help, if you want. Make some phone calls—"

Ian cut her off with a shake of his head. "What if he doesn't want anything to do with me?"

The stark vulnerability in Ian's eyes squeezed her heart and made it difficult to breathe. She had to whisper to keep her voice from breaking. "What if he does?"

His soft smile came slow, his eyes searching her face almost as if he were afraid to hope. He pulled her in and pressed a kiss to her forehead before tucking her back against his chest. "Ah, me bonnie lass," he said, "what if he does."

She stayed in his arms, both of them drawing comfort from their closeness. The lazy way his thumb traced small circles at her hip had her leaning into him. The salt and sea air still clung to his shirt, his skin, and she could almost hear the whoosh of the waves as they hit the shore.

The urge to tilt her head up, to taste the salt on his neck, to work her way across the stubble that marked his jaw until she could kiss those lips, breathe the same air that he did, tempted her to push the boundaries of their friendship. She shifted. Ian groaned as her hip pressed against his erection.

He took her hips in his hands and pushed her just far enough away to break contact. "Ignore that."

"Why would I want to?" Despite what her father thought, she wasn't a whore. Did she like sex? You bet. Was she afraid to admit it? Nope. But what she gave, she gave freely. She shifted back against him.

"*Cora,*" he had that fatherly tone. It should have turned her off, but somehow coming from him, it had the opposite effect, especially knowing she turned him on. "As pathetic as this sounds, you're the first real friend I've had in a very long time. A real friend wouldn't screw that up by trying to sleep with you."

———

Santa Fe.

Nothing but another weekend, another rodeo, another crap run.

The inability to get her father's confrontation out of her head didn't help.

"It's okay, boy. It's not your fault," Cora reassured Panache. "I'll get my shit together. Promise."

Panache snorted as Cora combed her fingers through his forelock and the gelding tucked back into his bag of hay. This horse had a heart the size of Texas, and it killed her that she kept letting him down.

That late at night, most everyone had turned in for the night, and only a select few banks of lights remained on in the barn. She plopped down on the bale of hay in front of Panache's stall and rested her forehead on her knees with Josephine's words ringing in her head. *You just need to get laid.*

Maybe Josephine was right. Maybe Cora should stop fighting the losses and instead, do something about it.

"Hey. You okay?"

Cora glanced up and roughstock man, Scottie Hines, dropped down on the bale beside her. He spit a wad of tobacco into the dirt. She gave him a wan smile. "Never better."

"I watched ya ride. Ain't nuthin' but a thang. Everyone has their tough spells. Ya gotta ride like it don't matter, like way back in the day when ya did it for fun."

"Yeah, well it was a lot more fun when I was winning. Panache keeps eyeballing me. I think he's worried his hay's gonna be in short supply if I don't get my head screwed on straight. He isn't far from wrong."

"You'll get there." The way Scottie said it, she almost believed him.

Almost.

"Thanks. That means a lot."

"You know..." Scottie was quiet a moment, then turned to her as if he had something he wanted to say, then decided against it. Exhausted, Cora didn't press the point. Scottie stood and hitched a thumb over his shoulder. "I gotta check the animals one last time before I hit the hay."

They said their goodbyes and Cora stepped out of the barn into the darkness. The night was crisp and clear, and her breath come out in puffs of white as she marched her determined ass over to Ian's trailer.

The Santa Fe rodeo grounds had some outbuildings with

electrical outlets, and Ian had parked away from everyone, so he could plug in his camper.

It had been more than three weeks since she and Josephine had mistakenly 'outed' Ian, and he'd been paying the price ever since. She'd apologized repeatedly. He'd accepted, repeatedly, but while they'd spent a lot of their downtime together, something remained off between them. Despite everything she'd tried, she couldn't completely kill the rumor.

Which only made what she had to ask Ian that much scarier.

But as scared as she was, she found the probability of her career slipping through her fingers even more terrifying.

Which made her desperate.

As she crossed the parking lot, the hairs on the back of her neck sprang to life. She stopped and listened, but all she heard was the occasional distant neigh of a horse, and the bellow of a bull. In a parking spot off to her right, Matty's parked truck rocked, the windows steamed up. From inside she heard a girl giggle, then groan.

That wasn't what had made her skin crawl. She picked up her pace, making a beeline for Ian's trailer. The light shone through his closed blinds as she stepped up to the camper and rapped her knuckles on his door, thankful she wouldn't have to wake him to make her request.

He did say he owed you one.

"It's open," Ian called out.

Here goes nothing.

She blew out a breath, pulled open the door, and stepped inside. Reclining on the bench seat at the dining table, Ian lay with a pillow behind his head, a strip of negatives in his hand, and a pack of ice on his bare ribs.

The plastic smile she'd manufactured, melted. "What happened to you?" Stupid question. She knew what happened. This was all her fault.

"I ran into Matty's fist. Twice." Ian's lips twisted. How could he find anything about getting beat up amusing?

"I'm so—"

Ian held up his hand to stop what had to be her sixty-fourth apology. He sat up and dropped the ice pack on the table. Goose-bumps covered his chest, and a dark purple bruise bloomed over his left side.

She shook off her jacket and slid onto the bench across from him. "Please tell me this is where you say, 'you should see the other guy.'"

Ian shrugged. He looked tired. Beat. The last few weeks hadn't been easy on him. It pissed her off that some of the people she'd considered friends were so narrow minded and bigoted. "I won't have to give up my street brawler membership card."

She accepted his beer and his not-so-subtle change of subject.

Something Ian had said came back to her, how not taking advantage of a vulnerable woman made him a gentleman, not gay. How he'd been pissed on her behalf at how she'd expected men to treat her badly at times.

Then and there, she knew she'd come to the right man. If anyone could help her get back on top, it would be Ian. She wanted it to be Ian. *Needed* it to be Ian.

Maybe it could help him out, too.

Seeing Ian in this different, more focused light, made her throat tight. Like some of those photos of his that he'd shown her, where the subject of the picture was crisp and in focus and the background was fuzzy and blurred. Making what mattered stand out.

Ian stood out.

Ian mattered.

This might be a great idea for her career, but she was

starting to think it wasn't such a great idea for her heart. "You're a good man, Ian Murphy."

He didn't respond, he just stared at her over the top of his beer as if she were a conundrum he couldn't puzzle out. "Not as good as you think."

She knew that to be untrue. Which made what she had to ask him even more awkward. She nibbled on her thumbnail.

"We're friends, right? You cook me breakfast sometimes, we stay up late and talk or play cards." She thought she knew the answer, but she wanted to be sure.

He glanced up at her, his scowl replaced by a reluctant grin. He nodded. "We shook on it."

Then his eyes narrowed, and his smile slipped as if he knew she was up to something but couldn't figure out what. "Where are you going with this?"

Instead of answering right away, she took two long swallows of beer. "Do you still owe me one? Or has this..." she waved her bottle in the general direction of his bruised ribs, "made us even?"

"This doesn't negate what I owe you. Because of you, I've made some connections and some friends. I've been behind the scenes for some spectacular shots I wouldn't have gotten otherwise. So yeah, I still owe you. Big time."

She rolled the bottle between her palms and made circular designs on the table top with the condensation. "I need to call in that favor."

"Name it." His eyes were soft and sincere. Here was a man with a heart of gold. A man of his word.

This was the best-worst idea she'd ever had. "I want you to have sex with me."

8

I WANT YOU TO HAVE SEX WITH ME.

Beer got sucked into Ian's windpipe. He choked. He sputtered. Pressure built behind his eyes and a vessel thrummed at his temple as he struggled to catch his breath.

Yanking the beer out of her hand, he set them out of her reach and cleared his throat. "Exactly how much have you had to drink tonight?"

She leaned across the table and snatched the beer back. "This is the first drink I've had all night."

"You're cr—"

She held up her hands, her eyes wide with some weird combination of panic and vulnerability and freaked-the-fuck-out. "Will you just hear me out?"

A swig of beer was his answer. He listened while she explained Josephine's theory on why she kept knocking down the barrels. All the while he tried not to think too much about what she was really asking, because the thought of having her in his arms, in his bed, made him hard.

His sweatpants wouldn't hide a thing. He glanced at the ice

96

pack but couldn't think of an inconspicuous way of dropping it in his lap without being obvious.

Her dark, wavy hair lay across her shoulders and she took a hunk of it in her hand and started playing with it, chewing on the inside of her cheek while she waited for his answer.

He'd like to think he paused to give the question—proposition? —the considerable thought it deserved. He'd like to think that he was thinking with his brain and not his dick, and he'd really like to believe that maybe she'd started to feel something for him. Even though the way she'd explained it made it perfectly clear this was nothing more than a transaction.

A payment on a debt.

Which stung more than a little.

"Let me get this straight," he said. "You want me to have sex with you because Josephine thinks you lost your groove, because you had a pregnancy scare and swore off men. Now you're in the middle of a sexual dry spell and hitting barrels and losing runs. Is that right?"

"It sounds worse when you say it like that."

"So, this is a no strings, no expectations, simple sex—"

"Unless you think you can't do it without falling for me because like I said—"

Ian cut her off. She didn't come off as conceited, just concerned.

"You don't do relationships."

"Exactly."

How many kinds of fucked up was it that he was even considering accepting her offer? He'd be a complete bastard to do it. Right? *Right?*

Cora fidgeted in her seat and she plucked at the label on her beer. "If it's my reputation that's turning you off, in my defense, my sex life has been *waaay* over exaggerated. You've experienced firsthand the staying power of the rodeo rumor mill. I learned early on you can't stop it. So, I stopped trying."

"You think I'm not taking you to bed because you've had sex with other men?"

She shrugged and sunk lower in the booth. Certainly, a woman like Cora wasn't used to rejection, but Ian was equally as certain she wasn't used to being cherished.

Like she deserved.

His veins heated as emotion flooded in. Jealous? Of the sex? No, he realized, pissed that the men in her life hadn't appreciated her for the sweet, sexy, funny, intelligent person that she was. "I've got news for you, babe. I don't care how many men you've slept with. I haven't exactly been a choir boy myself. It would be pretty hypocritical for me to judge you for having sex when I've done the same thing."

She sat up, hope flooding into her eyes. "Is that a yes?"

"No."

Yes.

No. No, no, no. Argh. That's not how he'd seen that little speech going. So much for letting her down easy. Now he'd gotten her hopes up. Time to change tactics. "Look, I don't like to start things I can't finish."

The declaration sounded lame even to his own ears, but the truth was he'd never been a 'one-and-done' kind of guy. What she asked for wasn't something he could give without falling deep for a girl who didn't do relationships.

"As soon as I get that assignment, I'm out of here."

As her eyes got glassy, she swallowed hard, and she nodded. She glanced up at the ceiling, a rueful laugh falling from her lips. "S-so that's a definite no then."

The silence built. He didn't know how to let her down any easier.

"This could help you too," she said, her tone saying she was grasping at straws, but didn't care. "Sleeping with me. When word gets out, it'll stop that gay rumor in its tracks."

"I don't kiss and tell. So, no. It wouldn't."

"Still..." Her voice had shrunk three sizes and she shrugged.

"Besides, we could just as easily kill the rumor with a lie."

"Maybe. But that wouldn't help me with my barrel problem."

Ian cradled his head in his hands. Lord help him, he was trying to be the good guy here, but even a good man had his limits.

"There are so many ways this can go wrong." He reached across the table for her hand and rubbed circles across her knuckles. "Look at me."

When she did, the vulnerability in her eyes ripped and tore at his heart. How on earth could anyone, could *he*, tell her no? "Cora, I win that contest, I'm leaving. I don't plan on coming back maybe for months or years or...or *ever*."

"I'm not asking for forever. I'm asking for now."

"Why me?"

She laughed—not that full bodied, full-of-life laugh that never ceased to make his heart feel full—and discreetly swiped at her eyes. "For the first time in my life, I don't want some random guy. You've been a good friend to me and you're trying so hard to say no. *That's* why I know it has to be you." Then her eyes cleared, and she screwed on a wily, seductive smile. "That, and because of your ass."

"My ass? Not my sparkling personality?"

"Well," she said, as if it were an afterthought, "that too."

Against his better judgement, but too tired to fight against something he'd wanted since he'd laid eyes on her at The Wheel, he said, "You sure about this?"

The full-bodied grin she gave had him reaching for his camera again. She swatted his hand away. "Enough with the pictures."

Chugging the last of his beer, he said, "Let's do this then."

He took her hand and led her toward the bed, knowing full well this could be something he would come to regret.

———

Cora followed Ian to his bed, filled with relief and nervousness, and gratitude and trepidation. But mostly relief.

Oh, and a little bit of lust.

A little?

Okay, fine. Make it a lot.

"So how do you want to do this?" She couldn't look him in the eye.

Why was she so shy all of a sudden? Usually confident and quick to strip, now for some reason her hands shook, her fingers fumbled with the buttons of her shirt, and her lungs had completely forgotten their vital job. Black spots dotted her vision. Ian caught her and sat her on the edge of the bed.

"Hey, now. You're not going to pass out on me, are you?"

"No." Her stomach flopped, but she refused to vomit. That would be one hell of a mood killer.

With a hand under her chin, he lifted her face to his and all she saw was an amazing, insightful man. He may not want her the way she wanted him, but on some level, he cared...perhaps more than anyone had in her past. She knew better than to dare ask for more.

She pulled in a lungful of air, and her vision cleared. "I'm okay. I'm here."

When she thought he might pull away, he dipped his head, going in for a kiss. She zigged left when she should have zagged right. His fingers got tangled in her hair. Their noses smashed together, and their teeth clacked. They both pulled back, laughing.

"Ouch." Her eyes watered as she checked her upper lip for blood. "I'm so sorry."

"'Tho kay," he muttered as he wiggled his front tooth, making sure she hadn't knocked it loose. "At least we got that awkward first kiss out of the way."

This encounter was more awkward than the first time she'd had sex in the cab of Jacob Stanham's tractor. Back then it had been all arms and legs. Steering wheels and stick shifts. Hormones and lust. Curiosity and impetuousness.

Not what was amounting to a business transaction.

No. Definitely not a business transaction, because she knew Ian would've have never said yes if that were the case, no matter how pretty he might think she was.

If she was honest with herself, she knew if she'd tried hard enough she could have found someone else willing to take her up on her offer, if all she'd wanted was a box ticked and an itch scratched.

But she didn't want Joe Blow. She wanted Ian.

Not just because he filled out his Wranglers better than most of the cowboys on or off the circuit.

Better make a move before he changes his mind.

Her fingers went back to her shirt, but he put a staying hand over hers.

"This isn't something we should have to force," he said. "It's not like we're on a time limit here."

Actually...

She checked his watch and did a quick mental calculation. "I've got fifteen hours and forty-three minutes until I have to get Panache warmed up for my race tomorrow night."

His pupils dilated. "There's a lot we can do in sixteen hours, lass."

When his voice went all low with that Irish brogue kicking

in, it made her core get all warm and squidgy, and her thoughts got all kinds of imaginative.

"Like—" She almost asked, 'like what?' but a jaw-cracking yawn cut her off. Heat rushed up her neck to her cheeks until flames threatened to *whoosh* out the top of her head. If he didn't have a fire extinguisher in the camper, they could be in some real trouble.

When it came to initiating sex, she hadn't felt this embarrassed and out of sorts in...well...*ever*.

What was this man doing to her? "I'm sor—"

His lips touched hers, cutting off yet another apology. The lightness of the kiss reached down deep. He didn't demand, he gave— in each gentle brush of his lips on hers. She tasted the hops on his lips, but she couldn't blame the alcohol for making her head spin.

Pulling back, he said, "You need to stop apologizing."

She covered her mouth with her hand to stifle another yawn.

With his hands on her shoulders, he held her at arm's length and gave her the once over. "Tell me the truth. How long has it been since you've had a decent night's sleep?"

Too long. Which wasn't an answer he'd ignore. So, she said, "A bit."

Her eyes darted to the jumbled blanket on his half-made bed, remembering that night a few weeks before when an almost complete stranger had made her feel safe and worthy.

He caught her staring. "Do you trust me?"

Since she'd known him, he'd done nothing but show her by what he said and what he did that he had more kindness, forgiveness, and integrity than most people she'd over known. "I do."

"Then let me take care of you."

What 'taking care of her' entailed, she didn't know, but if it involved those lips—and especially if it involved those lips all over her body—count her in. *Twice.*

"Sit."

She sat and managed to beat back another yawn.

He reached for the Mets T-shirt he'd let her borrow before.

"You kept the shirt I wore under your pillow?"

"Um..."

Grown men always looked so adorable when they blushed.

He shook out the shirt and laid it across his shoulder, unable to meet her eye. "Under my spare pillow. There's a difference."

"Uh, huh."

With practiced ease, he unbuttoned her shirt and peeled it off, but instead of staring at her openly, he averted his gaze.

"It's okay to look," she said. "You're going to see all of me anyway. Unless you plan on having sex with your eyes closed."

He met her eyes then, the hunger in them intense. Naked. A delicious chill ran down her spine. "I don't."

She hoped and prayed to every God she'd ever heard of— just to cover all the bases—that he'd lean in for another kiss and start working his way excruciatingly slowly down from there. Instead, the rat fink popped the Met's shirt over her head, fished her hands through the arm holes, and settled the hem of her shirt around her waist.

From her vantage point sitting on the bed, she had the best view of his pecs and wavy abs. She skimmed a trembling finger up his centerline, his skin soft and warm beneath her touch. "You seem to be a tad confused. We're supposed to be taking clothes off, not putting them back on."

"Patience, lass." As unaffected as he tried to sound, there was a part of him, a *large* part of him, pressing against his cotton sweats that couldn't hide her effect on him. "I'm trying to be good."

"I want you to be bad." She reached behind her, unsnapped

her bra and slipped it off under her shirt and tossed it away. A low groan escaped the back of his throat.

Reaching for her feet, he tugged off her boots and socks, then reached for her silver belt buckle. "This okay?" he asked as his knuckles brushed her belly.

Her stomach muscles fluttered, and she managed a nod. He dragged her jeans past her hips and down her legs, running feather-light fingertips down her thighs and over her calves. Her nerves went live, and the yawning fits died.

In fact, she might never yawn again.

He hitched his chin toward the bed. "Scoot back."

Finally.

Ian fiddled with the thermostat, shut off the light above the table, then crawled into bed beside her. She expected him to pounce, like all the other men had, but instead, he tugged her over to him until her head lay on his chest.

His arm came up, his fingers working their way through her hair, massaging the back of her head. Her eyes drifted closed, as she skimmed a hand down his torso, tracing the fine, fuzzy trail beneath his belly button. Her pinkie finger dipped beneath the waistband of his sweats, the long, hard tip of him already slick with precum.

He hissed in a breath and grabbed her wrist, but not before she got one more tortuous stroke across the head. Even though she couldn't see his expression in the dark, the rigidity in his body, and his shallow breaths told her everything she needed to know—he wanted her.

"Why'd you stop me?"

He moved her hand up to his chest and held it there. "Right now, you need sleep more than you need sex."

"But you're—"

"Fine." He kissed the top of her head as his hypnotic fingers worked their way across the base of her skull. She practically heard her eyes roll into the back of her head.

"I'm not that...that sleepy," she mumbled. At least she thought she mumbled. Maybe she just said that in her head because his fingers never stopped working their magic. All the muscles in her body went slack.

"Shhh."

How could she fall asleep when...wh...

She woke with a start to a loud bang outside the camper as someone tossed a trash bag full of glass bottles into the metal dumpster. Along with the convenience of the electricity at the outbuilding came the disadvantage of the close proximity to the trash.

Rolling onto her stomach, she braced herself on her elbows, and glanced down at Ian, his short hair going this way and that, his sleep hooded eyes on her. She wiped the small pool of her drool off his chest with the blanket. Apparently, she'd slept really well.

"Morning," she said as he raised his arms over his head.

His back arched into the stretch, putting his flat nipple level with her mouth. She couldn't *not* take advantage of the opportunity.

"Morn—*gurnph*." His hand came down on the back of her head and held her there. This time when her hand slipped south, he didn't stop her.

———

CORA'S HAND EASED BENEATH HIS WAISTBAND, AND FOR THE FIRST time since they'd climbed into bed, his eyes drifted closed. He'd lain awake all night while she'd slept in his arms, in a deep, restful, much needed sleep.

One thing he'd learned about Cora...she liked to snuggle.

Every time a soft sigh had escaped her mouth, or a toe raked up his leg, or her hands brushed his side, it had sent little shocks and salvos up and down his body.

Which meant he spent all night with a semi hard-on, his hand clenched to keep from shaking her awake and giving her what she'd so desperately wanted the night before.

He'd promised himself if she still wanted to have sex with him in the morning, he'd give up his Saint card. By the way her hand rubbed up and down his shaft, and the way her tongue laved, and her teeth nibbled at his nipple, she hadn't changed her mind.

Gently, he held the back of her head as she sucked and licked and drove him toward the edge. With her foot stomped down on the sexual gas pedal, he managed, "You still good with this?"

"Shut up. This is happening."

Then she froze, her grip still deliciously tight on his cock as she glanced up. The morning sun had risen enough that he could make out her features. Her dark hair lay in a tussle around her head, her brows raised as high as her hopes. "That is unless you don't want to. *Please* say you want to."

Fuck, yeah. Ian chuckled. "I want to."

"Good answer."

He rolled his hips as her thumb brushed across his tip. She smiled. A sexy as hell combination of relief and devilment that made him kick himself for stopping her the night before.

Up and down his sternum, she kissed a path, pausing long enough at his belly button to dip her tongue in, but she didn't detour for long.

She released him long enough to throw back the blanket and strip off his sweats. A cool rush of air hit his bare skin as she shifted sideways. Now her luscious ass lay within his easy reach.

The slow slide of his hand up the back of her thigh stalled when her mouth came down on him.

Sweet Mother Mary Joseph. "Awh, *fuuck*." His hand went to the tangle of hair covering her face and he gathered it out of the way. He'd spent the last couple weeks dreaming of her hot, wet mouth going down on him. No way would he miss his chance to watch it happen.

Talent backed up her enthusiasm. Her hands and her tongue were everywhere. On his balls, on his shaft. Stroking and sucking and shrinking his world to just him and her, the here and now.

He needed his hands on her. The reptilian part of his brain kicked in and he traced his fingers up her inner thigh. Slipping his hand under the edge of her panties, he slid a finger through the moisture gathering there. Rubbing his thumb over her nub, a moan ripped from the back of her throat. His balls tightened and for a beautiful, blissful second, his world went blank.

"Too close." He shifted away, his dick falling free of her warm mouth with a resounding pop.

He'd suffered too long for this not to end with him inside her. His lungs worked double time the way they did on his morning jogs, and, despite the chill inside the camper, a light sheen of sweat covered his chest.

Cora leaned across him, her pelvis lining up with his as she reached for her boot and tipped it over. A couple of condoms fell out. He palmed her ass and ground against her.

He hadn't come prepared. Getting laid had been the farthest thing from his mind when he'd packed for the trip.

Not that he'd complain. The fact that she'd brought condoms, that she took charge, that she took responsibility instead of leaving it all up to him, made her impossibly sexier.

Wiggling back onto the bed, she sat up, shucked her panties, and straddled him. So close to coming, he clamped his hands on her hips, pinning her pelvis in place. One false move and this thing would be over.

She tore the packet with her teeth and spit out the small corner. He needed a few minutes to bring himself back from the brink. "We're getting right to it? You don't want me returning the favor?"

"Next time."

His dick jumped.

The way her nose scrunched when she laughed then snorted made her impossible to resist.

"I'm glad a part of you likes that idea."

"All of me likes the idea of a next time."

He wrapped an arm around her waist and pulled her in for a kiss. Her mouth opened to his, her tongue darting out, fast and teasing. Spending a night or two with this woman would never be enough.

With her hips free, she took advantage and rocked against him. His head fell back, and Cora kissed and nibbled her way down his chin and across his jaw, the scrape of her teeth on tender skin shot goosebumps across his and down his arms.

She gave him a teasing, appraising look. "Last night, you weren't convinced."

"Last night I was an idiot."

She cocked her head and eyed him. "Why do you have a funny look on your face? You didn't expect me to argue with that, did you?"

Ian chuckled. "No. I don't suppose you would."

With a grin, that promised delightful, evil torture, she slid the condom from the wrapper. He went to take it from her, and she pulled her hand away. "I want to do it."

Who was he to disagree? He folded his hands behind his head to watch as Cora scooted back, giving herself better access. She held onto him, her grip bold.

With the condom pressed to his tip, she stopped. "To be clear, those rumors that I'd poked holes in a condom to try and get pregnant aren't true. But if you want to use your own, I'd understand. We can even double wrap. Plus, I'm on birth control now so—"

If he'd believed the rumors, he'd never would have taken her to his bed. Ian gave her thigh a gentle squeeze of comfort. "It's okay. I trust you."

In that split second before she smiled back, the old hurt, and ridicule flashed in her eyes. He doubted she'd ever admit how painful the rumors were. Though he loved that, at the same time, he didn't see any shame or apology. Here was a woman who gave society's conventional rules the big 'fuck you', refusing to let others dictate how she lived her life.

As much as he admired it, he also found it sexy as hell. You only got one shot at this thing called life, so it would be tragic to let other's opinions keep you from living it.

She eased the condom down. "You trust me, or *little Ian* trusts me?"

That sass. He grinned. "We both do."

"You with me?" She asked.

"All the way."

She shifted, placing him into position, and wasted no time sheathing him. "Um... *wow*..." She stilled, her breath coming in short, hot pants as her body clamped around him.

Those were his exact words. Only he couldn't say them because it took all his concentration to keep from groaning like a porn star. Ian held tight to her hips, realizing he'd made a terrible, terrible mistake letting her on top, giving her the control. Because in a few seconds he would lose his. He tried to think of unsexy things like f-stops and focal length and film speed. It helped some, but not enough.

"I take it back," she said.

His thumb slid to the top of her folds and she pressed against him. "What's that?"

"The 'little' comment. I'll have to come up with another name for your penis. Like the Incredible Bulk."

"Isn't that supposed to be Incredible Hulk?"

"Not in your case."

"Do you...*guh*..." Even with his hands on her hips, she didn't let that stop her from moving. He should have known nothing would keep Cora from getting exactly what she wanted. "...name all the penises?"

"Just the deserving ones."

He almost asked how many she'd named, but he didn't want to know the answer. He didn't begrudge her her past. He'd just rather not hear about it while she rode him.

"Aren't you going to take off my shirt." She threw on a coy, innocent look. He knew her well enough now to know neither could be used to describe her.

"You're trying to get me to let go of you."

"You say that like it's a bad thing."

She rounded her hips. His spine tingled, and his balls drew up and his voice came out tight when he said, "It is if you don't want this to last more than one-point-five seconds."

She stripped off her shirt, her eyes lighting when his gaze landed on her breasts. "Nothing wrong with a quick start."

Awh, hell. He had to touch her. She stilled when his hands brushed up her belly, her muscles clenching around him as he settled her breasts in the palms of his hands. He kneaded the abundant mounds, his thumbs brushing over her taut nipples. Her head fell back and rolled on her shoulders from side to side, as she rubbed and ground against him, chasing that sweet release.

Streaks of hot pleasure shot up his spine. He couldn't take it any longer. He wrapped his arm around her waist and reversed their positions. It wasn't the graceful roll he'd seen in the movies. His foot got caught in the covers, and he had to kick and fight to free himself. Cora's hand landed on his bruised ribs and for a split second the pain blocked out the pleasure.

He fell on top of her, barely able to catch his weight on his arms before crushing her, their bodies no longer joined, and their laughter shaking the mattress.

But that didn't dampen his lust for more.

9

———————

THE LAUGH ON CORA'S LIPS DIED WHEN IAN REACHED DOWN AND sheathed himself to the hilt. She couldn't remember when she'd felt so full, and it wasn't just because of the Incredible Bulk.

She was full of *him*.

Which turned her on even more. She let the low moan slip from her throat as she surged up against him. Cora needed more of this, of him.

Supporting his weight on his arms, Ian settled into a slow, sensuous rhythm. The cords in his neck strained along with his considerable control as he feathered kisses down her neck and across her shoulders until he found his way to her breasts. His stubble lit up her nerves and sent salvos of shivers down her spine.

Under the playful tug of his teeth on her nipples, she bucked, one hand cradling him to her breast while the other raked up his back as the pressure and pleasure built. Her breathing hitched, and all higher thought ceased as they galloped toward that soul-shattering cliff.

At the last second, he raised up, and she locked her legs behind him as he pounded into her. Flesh slapped. The camper shook. Hinges squeaked. An open cabinet door thumped and bumped.

"Faster," she said.

His breathing went raspy and rapid. He had to be near his limit.

Dropping back down on all fours, panting, sweaty and slick, as his strokes became erratic, he reached between them, brushing his thumb across her sensitized nub. Her nerves pinged, sending a rush of heat throughout her body. Cora clung to the edge of the cliff by her fingernails.

One slipped. Then the other.

She fell.

His name ripped from her lips at the same time they heard voices and the telltale clank of glass on metal as someone tossed a trash bag of their empties from the night before.

Ian covered her mouth with his, but he wasn't quick enough to keep her from crying out. His pace slowed, the rocking of the camper stopped, her climax squeezing around him. He thrust once, twice more. A low groan ripped from his throat as he stiffened above her.

After, he eased down to his forearms, his eyes meet hers, and she couldn't hold back the bubble of laughter. "Do you think they heard?"

Ian's face flushed, his chest heaving as he rolled onto his side and disposed of the condom. When he turned back to her, he said, "'They' as in the guys throwing their trash away or 'they' as in the parking lot in general? Because I'm pretty damn sure between the camper rocking and your screaming, the whole damn place knows."

"I'm sorry. I—"

For someone who normally didn't care what people thought, she hadn't apologized this much in almost all her life, but for some reason Ian's opinion mattered.

He rolled to his side and cupped his hand over her mouth and shut her up. Then he brushed his thumb across her cheek and pulled her in for a barely-there kiss that packed a power punch, touching her heart and tightening her chest.

"I told you to stop apologizing," Ian said. "I don't care who heard us. It's no one's business but our own."

"Maybe at least now the news will spread that you slept with me and people will leave you alone."

"I'm a big boy, Cora, I can fight my own fights."

Wait? Did he have a problem with her sticking up for him? She rose on an elbow. "Is that your way of saying you're too macho to have a woman fight your battles?"

With a hand to the back of her neck, he brought her in for another touch of his lips. A touch that gripped her heart in its tight fist. What was this man doing to her?

That part of her that would normally kick any kind of sentimental feelings in the balls and run screaming, wanted to wind a leg through his and pull him closer.

"I have nothin' against a lass fightin' me battles." The light sparked off his eyes as he laid the Irish brogue on extra thick and low. "In fact, I kinda fancy it. I'm just saying ye don't have ta, yeah?"

Heat pooled between her legs at the rumble of his accent. "I want to."

"Then I won't stop ye, lass." His fingertips worked the muscles at the base of her skull, making it almost impossible not to close her eyes and get lost in him again.

"You fight dirty, Ian Murphy," she mumbled, which only made her like him more. Want him more. "Do you always wield that accent like a sexual sword, making all the women want to fall on it?"

Okay maybe not all the women. Maybe just her.

"I don't care about other women," Ian said, his brogue gone. "All I care about is this one."

She started to shift away. This was supposed to be a simple hook up, a means to an end. Not anything more. It couldn't be anything more. They'd both made that clear.

He smoothed the crease between her brows, his other hand on her hip, keeping her from running. "Don't panic. I didn't mean anything by it. We both know what this is."

She wasn't panicking because she thought he might be developing feelings for *her*, she was panicking because she was developing feelings for *him*. Stupid. He was leaving. All the more reason to stick to rodeo cowboys.

He shifted her between his legs, the beginnings of his new-found arousal pressing against her lower belly. His hands slid down and cupped her ass. "How was it for you?"

By the wicked grin on his face, she knew he was up to something. "What kind of grading system are we looking at and how confident are you?"

His grin got impossibly wider. "What do you mean?"

She nipped at his bottom lip, at the stubble on his chin. "I can use a ten-point scale with decimals. A letter grade with pluses and minuses. Or, if you're scared, I could simply evaluate your performance on a pass/fail basis."

"All I need to know is if it was good enough to win a barrel race." His chuckle died with a hiss as she ground her pelvis against his.

She trailed kisses up his neck and across his jaw, whispering into his ear, "Maybe we should give it another go, just to be sure."

Ian rolled her over, a smooth, seamless motion with none of the fumbling awkwardness from before. He pressed a kiss between her breasts and started working his way down. "I think we should."

———

Fresh from Ian's shower, Cora stepped out of his trailer and into the mid-morning Santa Fe sun, her body buzzed, her smile dazzled, and the pleasant chafe between her legs let her know she'd been well and truly fucked.

She hurried to her trailer with a spring in her step and a simmering heat at her core that might keep her warm all winter long. As Cora rounded Josephine's trailer, Josephine stepped out.

"There you are." Josephine raised the small garbage bag in her hand. "I guess it's safe to toss this in the dumpster now."

Cora scoffed. "We weren't that bad."

With a bob of her chin, Josephine indicated the trailer next to them, a garbage bag lay on the ground by the door. The truck to Cora's right had a stack of empty beer cans stacked by the rear tire.

"Yeah, it was," Josephine said. "But if it makes you feel any better, two people already dropped out of the barrel race tonight, figuring they didn't have a shot now that your dry spell has ended."

Cora laughed. "Did not."

Josephine's sassy smile said otherwise, but Cora still didn't believe her. Josephine had kept her theory between the two of them—okay, and maybe Silas, but he was back at the Cox ranch where he didn't have anyone to tell.

"Soooo..." Josephine drew the word out and threaded her arm through Cora's as they headed to the barn to take care of the horses. "Was I right about all that runner's stamina?"

Josephine wanted the full scoop, but for once Cora didn't want to talk about her sexcapades. Cora gave Josephine's shoulder a bump with her own. "I don't kiss and tell."

"Ha. Since when?"

Cora shrugged, the heat making the slow climb up her neck and settling into her cheeks for what felt like the long haul. She may never have to wear blush again.

What she and Ian did, what they'd felt—not only in the physical sense, but the emotional as well— left her feeling raw and exposed, yet at the same time desired and cherished. She'd never known it could be like that, and she didn't want to share.

"Well?"

If Cora ever wanted another moment's peace, she would have to throw her friend a bone. "All I can say is it's a shame tonight isn't the money round."

Josephine squealed and wrapped Cora in a quick hug. A bunch of heads turned as they entered the barn, and Cora's left eardrum rang. "You're back. I know you are."

Cora reached for the latch on Panache's stall as Josephine reached for Comet's. "You and Comet better watch out, we'll be gunning for you."

"Damn," Josephine said, though the delight on her face never faltered. "You didn't say he was *that* good."

"Guess you'll just have to wait and see."

Hours later, the calm that had settled deep into Cora's bones after having sex with Ian still kept her mind clear and nerves settled. She warmed Panache up with the quiet confidence of a woman who knew with certainty she and her horse would finish with a qualifying round.

She felt it.

Panache felt it.

When her turn came, she lined Panache up at the end of the alley and nudged him into a gallop, the smile never leaving her face, because in a handful of seconds, everyone in those stands would know it too.

As Cora and Panache burst past the gate headed for the first barrel, the cheering of the crowd faded to a dull roar and dipped beneath the thump of her heart, the thunder his hooves.

Dust kicked up as they turned the first barrel, the speed of the run making her eyes water as they shot toward the second barrel. As she started to ease back on the reins, Panache rated his own speed and hugged the second barrel like a long-lost friend.

Cora didn't glance down, didn't fear spudding the barrel with her knee or scraping it with her stirrup. She left Panache to his job and focused on that third barrel, driving him faster.

With an extra nudge, Panache surged for the third barrel, digging into the turn, his legs scrambling, the dirt flying. On the run back to the finish line, her hat flew off as she stood in the stirrups, her reins and hands high up her horse's neck pushing harder.

Then the dark alley swallowed them whole, the scent of hot dogs, cotton candy, and stale beer buried beneath the intoxicating smell of victory.

Panache slowed and stopped as another horse and rider shot into the arena. Josephine rode over and slid off Comet. She pulled Cora out of the saddle and into a bear hug. "You did it!" When Cora's feet finally hit the ground, Josephine said, "Was I right, or was I right?"

Cora laughed at the good-natured I-told-you-so. She didn't have an issue admitting Josephine had it right all along. *Note to self—listen to Josephine.*

"Did you catch my time?" Cora asked.

"13.84," Josephine said. "It should hold unless Comet and I beat you." She wasn't bragging. Until Cora's dry spell, all their races had been neck and neck. Cora hated to lose, but if she had to be beat, she wanted it to be by her best friend.

Over the loud speaker they announced the arena drag and the next five competitors, with Josephine's name first on the list.

"You'd better go," Cora said. "I'm going to cool Panache down. We'll see you after."

"Congrats again."

"I owe you one." Cora turned toward Panache, wrapping her arms around his neck, breathing in the smell of dirt and sweaty horse. His sides still heaved from the run, but when she took his reins over his neck and led him down the concourse, he had a proud spring in his step that matched her own. *That* was how you ran a barrel race.

That's how you stayed in the money.

Now if only her good luck hump held.

"Cora," someone called out.

She glanced up expecting to see Ian jogging over to her to celebrate her run, but instead of Ian she saw Levi. She glanced around. No Ian. Tamping down on her disappointment, Cora accepted a quick hug from Levi.

"That was amaz—"

"There you are," Patty Bennett, Levi's newest girl and expert gossip said. She slipped her arm through Levi's and gave it a possessive tug. "What are you doing talking to her?"

Patty said it with a raised lip, the kind you get when you step in dog shit and are trying to figure out how to get the stench off.

Levi closed his eyes and blew out a breath before glancing back at Patty. "I was just—"

"You're with me now, remember? The one who *doesn't* poke holes in condoms."

I don't need this shit. Cora clucked to Panache, heading for the outdoor arena to cool him down. Levi put a staying hand on her arm, and to Patty said, "Give us a minute."

Cora hardly recognized Levi's thin tone, the one that said the normally laid-back man hung at the end of his tether by his teeth, his patience all but shattered.

Patty's glare went from Levi to Cora and back again. "You know she's with that photographer dude now, right?"

"*Enough.* You—" Levi cut himself off.

What a shame. Cora was dying to hear what he was going to say. Lucky for Patty, Levi wouldn't humiliate someone for the hell of it. Patty didn't deserve him.

"I'll meet you at the truck," Levi finally told Patty. When she'd left, he said to Cora, "You looking for Ian?"

Cora stopped her scan of the under-bleacher crowd. "What? No. I was just..." *Just looking for Ian.*

Ian had never said he'd see her after the race. He had his own work to do. His own dreams to chase. She knew his life didn't evolve around her. Still didn't mean that smidge of disappointment didn't curdle like spoiled milk in her belly.

"Sorry about Patty," Levi said. "She gets a little jealous."

"She has no reason to be jealous. You and I have been over for a while. We've both moved on."

"Yeah," Levi said, his eyes shifting, then came back. "About that. I was thinking, if things don't work out with—"

"There you are. I got your hat," Ian called out as he and his camera rounded a corner. He slung an arm around her neck and gave her a big smacking kiss on her temple, plopping her hat onto her head as little grains of arena dirt rained down. "You were a super star. I guess Josephine was right after all."

"Right about what?" Levi's tone fell flat, his gaze shifting between Cora and Ian as if either he hated being left out, or as if he hated being interrupted. Cora couldn't be sure.

"Oh, hey, Levi." Ian held out his hand. Then Ian must have clued in on Levi's body language, on the thin press of Levi's lips, on the hands on his hips and the granite gaze he'd leveled on Ian. "Ah, am I interrupting? I could—"

"Can you give us a minute?" Cora asked Ian.

"Naw. It's okay." Levi said, as he leaned in and gave Cora a peck on the cheek. "I need to go. I'm really happy for you, Cora. I just wanted to come congratulate you."

Cora watched Levi walk away. Had he been going to ask her to get back together? That would be nuts. They'd had a lot of good times together and he'd been a hell of a lot of fun in bed, yet even with that, there hadn't been real hurt feelings on her end after they'd broken up. That's how Cora knew that despite what a great catch Levi was, he was one fish she'd been glad had spit the hook.

Ian fell into step beside her and walked with her around and around the outside arena as Panache's breathing slowed and his sweat dried. Around them, other riders warmed up and cooled down their mounts.

"I've got a question about this sex theory of Josephine's," Ian asked after they'd made several rounds.

"What's that?"

"Is it a one and done thing? Like you don't need me anymore because you're cured?" Was that disappointment in his voice? Then he got this criminally cocky smile. A smile that made her insides quiver and made her want to climb his body like a stripper pole. "Or will there be a need for... ongoing maintenance?"

Cora stopped abruptly, and a rider skirted to the side, with an irritated, "On your left."

She took Ian's hand and dragged him from the arena and over by one of the paddocks holding the roping steers. A scraggly patch of frost-burned grass lined the fence and Panache started munching.

Leaning back against the rails, she said, "Like all high-performance equipment, I'm afraid occasional maintenance may be required."

Ian stepped between her legs and lifted the hat off her head, his voice low and near her ear when he said, "Lucky for you I was a grease monkey in my previous life. I can keep you lubed up…"

He traced his tongue across her bottom lip, making her breath hitch. "I can keep your wheels spinning…"

He ducked back in for another quick taste, with a teasing flick of his tongue. She groaned, and her hands went to his hips, guiding him until she could straddle his leg. "Your engine humming…"

He cupped her ass forcing her up his thigh, the friction making her already damp panties soaking wet. "…and keep your fluid levels at max."

She broke the kiss long enough to say, "You'd do that for me?"

"Well, you are my friend."

Cora chuckled. "I should thank you."

"Trust me," he said, slipping into the brogue he knew pressed all her go-go buttons and ignited the afterburners. "It's me pleasure, lass."

10

After Ian got his shots in of the saddle bronc and bull rides, he and Cora met back up. Now he was keeping Cora company while she swapped a stall cleaning for a flake of alfalfa to treat Panache for what turned out to be the winning run for the night to put her in the Sunday finals.

"I sold a few photos to riders this week, I can loan you—"

"I don't want your money." Then she tossed him a saucy grin. "I won't need it as long as your magical, race-winning, penis lasts."

"Fair enough." Ian chuckled. "I can grab another manure fork and help?" Ian leaned against the stall door, feeling useless. "I don't mind."

Cora sifted through the shavings and plopped a forkful of poop into the wheel barrow. "I'm almost done, but thanks."

When she finished, he followed her to Panache's stall. At least this time she allowed him to help brush her horse out.

Cora used a rubber curry comb to break up the dried sweat on her horse while Panache devoured his treat with the enthusiasm of a kid left alone with a sheet cake. Ian could practically hear the horse's lips smacking.

On the opposite side of the horse, Ian used the soft body brush and flicked away the sweat and dirt she had loosened. He sneezed at the cloud of dirt and dander he'd raised.

"Such a city boy," Cora teased. "I guess it's a good thing you don't plan on sticking around."

His steady strokes faltered, then picked back up again. Why didn't he like being reminded that he was leaving? Why were the weeks, the days, the hours, the minutes, going by faster, faster, faster?

For the first time in his life he wanted time to slow way down, when he should want things to speed up. After all, the opportunity this contest could bring had been his dream for years now.

"Speaking of leaving, I'll be sending in my photos and essay for the first-round tomorrow. Then I have to call the magazine in a week to see if I'm one of the finalists."

"Then how much longer after that until you know if you've won?" Cora's voice went soft, as if she were afraid to ask.

Ian's voice didn't come out much stronger, just as afraid to answer. "If I'm a finalist, I'll have to send them one more photo essay. Then they'll choose from the final submittals. So, we're maybe looking at two to three weeks, tops."

Cora fell silent. All he heard was the scraping of the currycomb against the dried sweat and the soft munching of hay.

At the clomp of approaching boots, Cora glanced up. Scottie Hines paused at the stall opening, his face falling when he caught sight of Ian. "Sorry. I didn't know you had... company." He backed away and started down the aisle.

Tossing the currycomb aside, Cora ducked under Panache's neck and went after Scottie. "Hey, wait up."

Ian watched through the bars dividing the tops of the stalls.

Cora put a staying at hand on Hines' arm to get him to stop. Even then the stockman wouldn't look at her.

"Did you need something?" she asked Scottie.

"No...I just..." Hines hitched a thumb over his shoulder toward the outdoor paddocks where a lot of the roughstock had been placed for the rodeo. "I better check on the animals one last time before I turn in for the night. Congrats on your run. You deserve it."

"Thanks, I'm –"

Ian turned back to the horse, not wanting to eavesdrop, but convinced Scottie had hoped to find Cora alone.

He couldn't blame the man.

But tough shit. There was no way, no how, that Ian would give her up before he had to. He would be out of her life soon enough, and then her heart would be up for grabs.

He finished brushing Panache. When she returned to the stall he said, "Everything okay?" as innocently and naturally as he could without sounding nosy or jealous. It wasn't easy to pull off.

"Yeah, sure." But she had this look on her face that said she didn't quite believe it. "Scottie just seemed a little off is all. But he's a hard man to get to know. More of a listener than a talker."

It was late, so they quickly finished up, Cora filling up Panache's hay bag, while Ian dumped the heavy water bucket and returned with fresh water. Cora gave Panache a scratch on the withers and a kiss on the end of his soft nose before telling her racing partner good night.

They took the scenic route back to her trailer. Walking along the outskirts of the parking lot where the lights didn't quite reach, and the stars shined bright.

The cool air invigorated him, or maybe what made his blood flow and his heart beat double time was the fact that the most beautiful woman he'd ever known walked beside him, their fingers linked, their shoulders brushing.

"So how was your night?" Cora asked. "Did you get some good shots?"

"I think so. I'll know for sure once I can get a good look at the negatives. Thanks again for introducing me to Silas, and for helping me get behind the chutes. There's no way I could've gotten those shots, gotten that close, without him putting in a good word for me."

"Silas is a shirt-off-his-back kind of guy, and aside from a few phobic assholes, most everyone here would do whatever they can to help." They walked a little further, and Cora asked, "So, did the sex help you out tonight as much as it helped me?"

Ian shrugged noncommittally. If you could call angry looks and name-calling better than before, then yeah it had been better. At least no one took a swing at him. "Some maybe. I think we killed the gay thing for the most part, but now that most of the guys know I'm straight, now I'm the competition."

"Men are such idiots." Cora bumped him with her hip. "No offense. Present company mostly excluded."

"Gee, thanks." The way he'd been thinking with his dick lately, he didn't see how Cora could exclude him.

They made a turn back toward the parking lot near the dumpster, and as much as he wanted to take her back to his trailer and strip her naked and see how loud he could make her scream, he wouldn't. If she wanted sex, she'd have to come to him, already knowing his dick threatened to get his heart hooked too deep. They passed his trailer and headed back toward Cora's.

"Ignore those guys," Cora said. "Those guys who are giving you a hard time, are the same guys who were afraid to have a beer with me—even talk to me—after my scare, as if I could somehow get pregnant and trap them, just by sharing a drink.

Now that they see someone else might be interested, they're like dogs on a bone, snapping and snarling and generally being big, fat, hairy dicks."

"I won't argue with that."

By the time they'd made it back to her trailer, most everyone had settled in for the night, even Josephine appeared to be asleep.

Ian reconsidered his idea of waiting for Cora to come to him and was about to conjure up some cheesy excuse for her to spend the night with him, as if his magical dick would keep her in the money. Because the truth was, he liked having her in his bed, liked waking up with her in the morning, liked watching her nose crinkle when she laughed, and feeling her body shudder beneath his touch. More than he should. More than he ever thought he would.

He opened his mouth, hoping something funny or convincing or cocky would fall from his lips, anything but the truth.

That he wanted *her*.

"Uh, oh." Cora pulled her hand free from his.

"What's wr—" The words died on Ian's lips as he glanced past Cora. A piece of paper and another rose had been placed on the step of the trailer. He reached for it. Something in the back of his brain told him to stand up and take notice, but it felt too much like jealousy to be totally believed. "Your secret admirer strikes again."

Cora took the piece of paper and the wilted rose from his hand, her eyes scanning the parking lot, but if Ian had to guess, whoever had laid those on the steps would be long gone.

He turned on his camera flash to strobe mode to get a better look. "Jesus…"

"What did he do to my eyes?" Cora asked as a visible shiver

went through her. "Is this someone's idea of a sick joke? Because I'm not laughing anymore."

Far from fresh, the wilted rose petals had blackened around the edges. The piece of paper was a clipping of the photo of Cora dancing on the tables at The Wagon Wheel with holes poked in the shadows of her face where her eyes should be. He took it from her hand to get a better look.

"Throw it away," she said as she grabbed for it.

Ian held it out of her reach, afraid she'd crumple it up. "Hang on. This is getting out of hand. Maybe we need to call in the sheriff or—"

"What can the sheriff do? It's not against the law to leave someone flowers and a newspaper clipping."

"Maybe not, but I don't like some asshole creeping around your trailer in the middle of the night. Especially when all it would take is a well-placed screwdriver to pop the lock on your trailer to get to you."

"I don't think someone is trying to hurt me, I think—"

The trailer door clicked open and Josephine stuck her head out, her hair all mussed around her head. "I think you two need to keep it down, the rest of us are trying to sleep."

Ian shined his light on the rose and the newspaper. "Someone left this on your step."

"What? When?" Josephine pulled the corners of her blanket tighter around her. "It wasn't there when I went to bed. I never heard a thing."

"We should at least go check with rodeo security." Ian wasn't about to let this drop. Not when it involved Cora's safety. "Maybe one of their guys saw something."

"Hang on," Josephine said, "I'll get dressed and come with you."

It took some time, but Ian, Cora, and Josephine finally

tracked down one of the security guards who'd camped out at the rodeo office next to a fresh pot of coffee.

When they showed the guard the newspaper clipping, and the dead rose, he didn't get very excited.

"What do you expect me to do? There's only two of us. We can't be everywhere all the time. If you want my advice, I would find somewhere else to sleep until this nut job gets tired of the game."

"Are you freaking kidding me?" Josephine said. "You can at least put your damn coffee down long enough to patrol the parking lot. What are you gonna tell your boss when someone gets hurt? That you had a coffee emergency or that you were too lazy to give a flying fuck?"

"No one's going to get hurt." The guard took a lazy slurp of his coffee. "Whoever left this is not the type of guy that confronts you, he's the type of guy who scurries around in the dark like a cockroach, running for cover as soon as someone flips on the lights."

The prick was no help, and Ian refused to waste one more second with an incompetent security guard. "Come on," Ian said to the girls. To the security officer he let his tone go flat. "Thanks, man, you've been a great help."

"Yeah? Well, fuck you too buddy."

As they headed back to Cora's trailer, Ian said, "I want both of you to stay with me for tonight at least. There's plenty of room for the three of us. Tomorrow we can come up with a better solution."

"Pass," Josephine said. "I'm not staying in your trailer. All that rocking and rolling that goes on in there will make me seasick."

"I'll sleep in the dining area." Ian didn't care about the sleeping arrangements, all he wanted was Cora safe. "You two can share the back bed."

"And be responsible for Cora losing out on winning a check tomorrow night? Are you kidding me? I'll find somewhere else to stay tonight. You two have fun."

"Wait a minute here." Cora grabbed Josephine's arm before she could escape. "I don't get a say in all of this?"

"As long as it's 'yes,'" Ian said, "'for sure', or 'that sounds like a great idea', then yeah, you have a say." No way would Ian let Cora win this argument.

"That is our trailer." Cora's voice skipped two rungs up the octave ladder. "I'm not gonna let some numb nuts scare me out of my home. Besides, it's not like I'm going to be hard to find half a parking lot over in your trailer."

Cora didn't need to know Ian was seconds away from throwing her over his shoulder and going all small-minded, big-muscled caveman on her. He could almost feel the Neanderthal brow ridge forming above his eyes even as he moderated his tone. "Maybe not, but at my trailer, they'll have to go through me to get to you."

"Ian's right," Josephine said. "Don't be stupid. More than likely you're right and this won't escalate, but we don't know that. I want you safe. Promise me you'll stay with him."

"Jesus." Cora huffed out and exasperated breath. "Fiiine."

Ian and Cora accompanied Josephine to Mabel's trailer on the far side of the parking lot. The lights shone through the thin curtains, Mabel's shadow visible through the window. They knocked, and Mabel was more than happy to have a bunk mate for the night. They said their goodbyes, and Cora and Ian headed back to Ian's trailer.

"Do you have any idea who this bastard is?" Ian asked as he unlocked his trailer. He pulled the camera strap from around his neck and laid his camera on the table and plopped down on the bench seat. The Naugahyde cushion hissed under his weight.

Cora took the seat across from him. "Who says it's a guy?

Maybe it's one of the girls. Someone who's jealous. One of the barrel racers who lost tonight, or hell, even Patty for that matter. She didn't seem too happy that Levi came over to congratulate me."

"But it's the same clipping and the same type of flower as before. It would be too much of a coincidence that two people would send you those."

In Ian's experience, jealous women didn't hide. They came right up to your face and confronted you, all high-pitched voices, pointed fingers, and indignant accusations. This was a man. A jealous man. Now an angry man. If Ian ever got his hands on the rat bastard, the guy would be lucky to come out alive.

"Any guys you hooked up with that wish you two were still together?"

"Is this your sly way of getting a list of all the men I've slept with?"

Humor sparked in her eyes, and Ian had to admire the fact that she could joke around at a time like this. "Is that your sly way of letting me know the list is very long?"

"After the pregnancy scare, I can guarantee that the list of men who wished they were still with me has shrunk dramatically. But honestly, even before that, for the most part I've always remained friends after breakups. The guys I've been with knew what they were getting into when they slept with me. Simple sex. No harm. No foul. Just two people sharing their bodies and a good time. They weren't looking for anything serious any more than I was." Cora held her hands out wide. "Now, no one's interested in getting a piece of me."

"Present company excluded."

"Thank you for that, by the way." The humor had left her voice, replaced by sincerity. "For stepping up to the plate, so to speak."

"I seem to recall enjoying myself last night as much is you. Trust me, there's no need to thank me."

In fact, she probably wouldn't be thanking him if she had any idea how his thinking had shifted, how he'd tried to think of what he could say, how he might ask her if she wanted to come along with him if he won.

An impossibility he knew, but that didn't keep him from wishing things were different.

Cora's eyes got glassy, and she waved her hand in front of her face, as if she could wave the tears away. "Jeez. I don't know what's wrong with me. I'm just—"

"Exhausted." Ian slid out of the booth, taking Cora's hand, and helping her to her feet. Slowly he walked her backwards until the edge of the bed caught her on the back of her legs. "And stressed, and scared, and all those other things you should be feeling when someone has violated your sense of security the way that that person has."

Ian fluffed his pillow and pulled down the covers, helping her off with her clothes and into his Mets shirt. Handing her into the bed, he pressed a kiss to the top of her head. She smelled of arena dust and pine shavings. A mixture of scents that Cora had somehow turned into an aphrodisiac.

"Get some sleep, Cora. Tomorrow we can make a list of potential suspects, and maybe get to the bottom of this."

He tucked the covers around her and took a step back. She grabbed his wrist.

"Come to bed," she said. "We could both use some sleep."

Bending down, Ian skimmed a soft kiss on her lips, and brushed her cheek with a pad of his thumb, fighting the urge to say, 'the hell with it' and stripping down and falling into bed with her.

"Trust me," Ian said, "I would love nothing more, but those negatives won't develop themselves. I still have to find the shots I want to send into the magazine and write my story. I'll come to bed in a little bit."

"Ian," Cora tucked her hands under her chin and burrowed her head into the pillow. "Even though we're just friends, thank you for making me believe that I matter."

"You more than matter, Cora Hayes."

Because he didn't think he would ever get enough of her, he leaned in for another kiss.

As much as he wanted to make her his again, and again, and again, he had work to do. He couldn't let a woman, even Cora, get in the way of his dream.

Hours and hours later, Ian climbed into bed with gritty eyes, a tired back, and the realization that he might actually have a decent shot at winning the contest. That this dream of his could materialize, that he could grab hold and let it take him for a ride.

The photo essay he'd created for the editors at *GlobeTrotter Magazine* told a story few rodeo enthusiasts, much less the rest of the world, ever saw.

It wasn't the usual triumphant story of man conquering beast, but a story of bigotry and hate. Not smiles and waving hats at the cheering crowds, but sneers and clenched fists at the things that scared people the most.

Instead of acceptance and understanding, a fear and loathing of what was different. To be fair, that dark side of the rodeo didn't describe everyone, the vast majority, or even a small percentage. It described a handful of small-minded people—a tiny puss-filled boil on the hairy ass of humanity.

When people didn't understand, they got scared.

When they got scared, they hated.

When they hated, they fought back.

When they fought back, they were blinded and couldn't see the truth. The truth that despite all the differences, we were all running in the same race...

The human race.

He felt proud of the piece he'd created, but beyond the pride, beneath the exhaustion, sat a very heavy, glaring reality—this little thing with Cora, this friendship, or relationship or whatever the hell you called something that you didn't want to end—had a fast approaching expiration date.

———

CORA DIDN'T KNOW WHAT TIME IAN FINALLY CRAWLED INTO BED, but when she cracked an eye, the early morning light had started filtering in through the cracks around the blinds. She rolled over, and snuggled up against him, her front to his back.

Immediately, her mind rewound to the night before, to the newspaper clipping, to the dead rose, but she shoved it out of her head. There would be plenty of time to worry about that. Right now, all she wanted to think about was the way a certain photographer could make her body sing and her mind go blissfully blank.

She slipped a hand around his waist, her fingers skimming up the ripple of muscle on his abdomen. Goosebumps erupted beneath her fingertips, tiny blips of sinful pleasure.

A sound escaped the back of his throat that had her pulling him in tighter. His hand captured hers. "What are you doing?"

She pressed a kiss to his shoulder blade and slid her hand out from beneath his, skimming it back down his abdomen, following the trickling trail of hair around his belly button until her fingers slipped under the waistband of his sweats.

He never stopped her.

Instead, his hand reached back and palmed the back of her head, holding her lips against him. His pelvis rocked into her touch. "Jesus, that feels—"

Whatever he'd been about to say disappeared beneath a

deep, throaty groan that had her nerves buzzing and her leg looping over his, encouraging him to roll over.

She wanted his hands on her, his lips on her, his warm skin against her own. Stroking up the hard length of him, she smoothed the drop of precum over his tip. Beneath the scent of musk, sat the tangy undertones of developer and fixer, the tools of his trade much like dirt, hay, and horse sweat were hers.

How their two worlds fit together she didn't know. What she did know was that this man filled a hole inside of her that she hadn't known existed. He filled it to overflowing, planting deep rich grass and blooming fragrant flowers on a once tumbleweed filled landscape.

With him she felt safe, felt adored, felt like it wasn't just her against the world. As much as she wanted to sink into that world where she could let go and let him take over, she knew she couldn't become dependent on the temporary.

But that didn't mean she couldn't dip her toes into the wonderful world of Ian, at least for the time being.

He woke up in degrees, the fog of sleep deprivation lifting layer by layer as his cock grew harder and harder. Shucking his sweats, he rolled on top of her, pressing his pelvis against hers, her panties already damp.

"Morning, sunshine," he murmured in her ear. "You're up early."

His cock pressed against her belly. If there wasn't a layer of cotton between them she would have shifted and had him inside her in one smooth motion. She rolled her hips, his groan coming out more of a growl.

"Looks like Little Ian is up as well," she said.

"Little Ian?" He raised up on his arms, fighting a smile. "What is this compulsion about naming my penis?"

"What else am I supposed to call it?"

"Um...a penis?"

"That's not very original."

He pulled off her T-shirt, her breath catching when his mouth came down over a breast, his teeth lightly raking across her nipple. Whatever new name she'd been thinking of evaporated in a sea of sensations. She fisted her hands in his hair, holding him close as he worked his way south.

"The Bone Ranger," she managed.

She squeaked when he nipped her inner thigh. "No."

With a slow, practiced ease, he disposed of her panties. As much as she liked foreplay, there was something to be said for getting down to business. She tried to pull him back up, but the man was nothing if not determined.

He spread her legs and her back arched, anticipating his touch. His tongue flicked across her, and a lick of flames raced up her spine. "K-King Dong."

His lips settled around her clit, the rumble of his laugh making her even more wet and slick. He glanced up at her, giving her one more teasing lick. "Absolutely not."

He went back to work, his hands under her ass lifting her up to feast.

"I-Ian?"

His 'yeah' came out muffled.

"Don't make me beg."

With one last kiss to the inside of her thigh, he found a condom and slipped it on, bearing his weight on his arms as he positioned himself, his tip pressing tightly up against her.

"Mr.—" He kissed her before she could say another name, and she tasted herself on his lips. Grabbing his ass, she sheathed him, blowing out a huff of air as he stretched and filled her. "Perrrfect."

He hissed in a breath, his body still and stiff as he buried his face in the crook of her neck. He rolled his hips, soft and slow.

She tried to increase the pace, but he held fast, raising up on his arms so he could get a better look at her. "Mr. Perfect?" A splash of humor and a dash of mischievousness danced in his eyes. "Aw, lass. You are me treasure."

The brogue brushed against her, a soft caress he wielded like a vanquishing sword, but the declaration that she was his, was a direct hit to her heart. It was the first time he'd claimed her.

She liked the sound of that way more than she should have.

He must have read the vulnerability on her face as fear, because he brushed his thumb across her cheek and said, "No worries, lass. I aim to keep ye safe."

While she considered the slim possibility that some wacko might actually want to hurt her, the reality that Ian would break her heart when he left was inevitable.

So, no. There was no way he could keep her safe from heartache.

"I know." She cupped his cheeks and brought him in for a kiss, her tongue darting in, testing, tasting as the kiss deepened. Ian picked up the pace, driving harder and deeper as if he too could feel the building emotional desperation.

It fueled him.

It fueled them.

The trailer got to rocking and the cabinet got to banging again, but as her nerve endings pinged and the blood pooled at her core, she didn't care who knew or heard.

He raised up on his knees, his hands on her hips as he drove into her, his breath coming in harsh, staccato pants. So close. She reached down to touch herself, but he beat her to it, his thumb brushing through her wet folds until he found her nub. Her head fell back, her breasts bouncing to the rapid rhythm as she shot over the edge.

She clamped her heels around the back of his thighs, pulling him tighter against her as her internal muscles clamped down around him.

"Fuuuck," Ian ground out, his teeth clenched, the cords in his neck bulging out in sharp relief.

He dropped down to his forearms as his pace faltered, and he came. She held him tightly to her as they both caught their breath and their heart rates dropped below the red line.

Even with the chill in the trailer, the sweat stuck their bodies together, and though Ian's weight pinned her down, she had no desire for him to move. When he went to roll off her, she held him tighter.

"I don't want to crush you."

"Don't go," she insisted.

"We can't stay like this forever."

"Not forever. Just for now."

Cora had no doubt he'd crush her, but not from his weight. How had she gone from wanting a fast and casual fuck to get her head straight and win a few checks, to wanting much more than he had to offer?

The shitty thing was, he'd warned her ahead of time that he didn't want anything other than a friendship, and she didn't want to be the one to break their established rules.

After all, the sex had been her brilliant idea. So, when Cupid thought it would be hilarious to shoot her heart with a flaming arrow, she only had herself to blame.

11

Ian brushed the lock of sweaty hair away from Cora's face, loving the way the flush of sex still heated her body. Residual shocks from her climax contracted her walls around his semi-hard cock.

As sex partners, they had similar appetites. While they both enjoyed the slow and sensuous, she was also game when he got rougher. Her hands, her body, her words. All encouraging, all urging him harder and faster.

He raised up, blowing cool air across her sweat slicked breasts, peaking her nipples.

"Mmm," he said as he sucked on her breast. The slow way her fingers slid up and down on either side of his spine made goosebumps rush across his back, and smelling himself on her skin started making him hard all over again.

"Someone's energetic this morning," Cora said, thrusting up against him. "Ready for round two?"

"Oh, hell yeah. Just give me a minute." He nipped at her jaw and had just reached down to take care of the condom when there came a knock on his door.

Instead of looking horrified, Cora grinned. "Please tell me you remembered to lock the door last night."

He had. Probably. Maybe.

He glanced at the door, he couldn't tell if the lock was flipped from where they lay. Maybe if they stayed quiet no one would know they were there.

The knock came again. *Or not.* "Open up. I know you're in there."

"You gotta be fucking kidding me," Ian mumbled in her ear.

"What's Levi doing here?"

Bam, bam, bam. Hell if he knew. If Levi wanted his old girl-friend back, he was shit out of luck.

"You're gonna have to stop that," he groaned, as Cora wiggled beneath him. All he wanted was to sink balls deep back into her and forget the rest of the world existed. But having someone pounding at his door worked against a sustainable erection.

"Go away," Ian hollered.

"Answer the door."

Fuck. "Hold on to your ass, Banks."

Ian pressed a kiss between her breasts and pushed off the bed. Not because he wanted to, but because he had to. He threw on a pair of sweats and padded over to the door, tying the string at his waist.

His trailer smelled of musk and sex, reminding him what Levi was making him miss. Ian didn't bother hiding his irritation when he shoved the door open. "*What?*"

"The kids' mini-bull riding clinic is this morning. Thought you wanted pictures." Levi stood with his thumbs in the front belt loops of his jeans, his cowboy hat low on his head, his eyes averted.

Ian scratched his bare chest. If Levi had a problem with him sleeping with Cora, the placid expression the man had screwed onto his face did a damn fine job of hiding it. For a split second,

Ian wondered if Levi could be behind the flowers and the clippings. He'd have to talk to Cora about it as soon as he finished with the shoot that morning.

"Yeah, give me a sec," Ian said to Levi. "Want me to meet you at the arena?"

"I'll wait. I'm not in that big of a rush."

He closed the door and turned back to Cora. "I gotta go."

"I need to feed Panache, anyway," Cora said, though she didn't make any move to leave his warm bed.

Climbing back into bed and telling Levi to hell with it seemed like a viable option, but he didn't want to miss his opportunity to photograph the kids' clinic.

Ian shucked his sweats and turned on the shower. He didn't want to keep Levi waiting so he didn't bother switching on the water heater and waiting for the tank to warm up.

Besides, he'd need all the cold water he could get with the image of Cora laying in his bed, the blanket tucked up under her arms, her hair tussled, her lips plump, looking sated and freshly fucked.

Before stepping in the shower, he said, "I don't want you running around here alone until we have a better idea of who this idiot is who's targeting you."

Cora made a face, somewhere between drinking sour milk and no-fucking-way. "That doesn't exactly work for me. What are you going to do, keep me on a leash?"

He left the bathroom door open and raised his voice to be heard. "If I have to."

The cold water sluiced down his body, but it did little to ease his arousal. He washed, rinsed, dried, and dressed in record time. Under Cora's watchful eye, he slipped on his boots, grabbed his gear, and palmed his hat.

Before he left, he patted her hip and leaned in for a kiss.

"Please don't fight me on this. I don't want to have to worry about you while I'm working."

He opened the door and then realized she hadn't answered him. Did she think she could get away with ignoring his request if she didn't answer in the affirmative?

"Promise me you'll stay with Josephine or someone else that you trust."

Her eyes narrowed. "You're not my father."

No. But the challenging way she stared at him made him want to bend her over his knee and give her a spanking.

Knowing her, she'd probably enjoy it as much as he would.

"You coming already?" Levi grumbled, his patience running thin. "If I'd known you'd take that long I'd have met you at the arena."

"I'm coming."

Ian clomped down the step and ducked his head back in the trailer. He wouldn't leave unless she acquiesced. All he needed was a little leverage for her to agree. "Lock up behind me. I'll stop by your trailer and send Josephine over. And FYI, if you ever want a visit from *Mr. Perfect* again, you'll humor me."

Cora cracked a reluctant smile. "You can't hold sex hostage."

"Watch me."

He closed the door and turned to find Levi choking down a laugh.

Ian fell into step beside him. "What's so damn funny?"

"Mr. Perfect?"

Hell. "You didn't hear that."

"Um, yeah. Pretty sure I did." That time Levi couldn't hold back the chuckle.

"Shut the fuck up," Ian growled, but that only made Levi laugh harder.

Ian stopped by Josephine's trailer. She was back after spending the night with Mabel and she promised to pick Cora up and go with her to the barn to feed. On the walk over to the arena, he and Levi fell into an awkward silence. Ian shouldn't feel weird sleeping with Cora, after all, Levi had no claim on her, but over the past few weeks he and Levi and become friends and he didn't want any bad blood.

They stepped beneath the stands on the way to the chutes. This time of morning, the chutes were normally quiet, but even at a distance, the sounds of kids talking and laughing spilled over the fences onto the concourse. The miniature bulls mooed, and the pungent odor of cow shit and piss lay thick beneath the stands.

"We need to talk." Ian put a staying hand on Levi's arm. They stopped near a support column.

"What?" By the way Levi crossed his arms over his chest, and the set of the man's jaw, Ian figured Levi had a pretty good idea what he was about to say.

Ian didn't hem or haw. Levi and Cora had a history, and even if their relationship had ended in Cora's mind, Levi could feel different. Looking the bulldogger straight in the eye, Ian asked, "Do you have a problem with me seeing Cora?"

"Doesn't matter what I or anyone else wants. Cora's her own woman."

"That doesn't answer the question."

Levi dug his fists into his pockets, a resigned half-smile on his face. "If she's happy, then I'm happy."

Ian held Levi's gaze for a second. Two. Then Levi hitched his thumb toward the arena. "Kids are waiting."

Levi started walking and Ian followed, still cognizant of Levi's non-answer and the fact that whatever half-response Ian had gotten, Levi could be lying through his ass. But something in what the man had said rang true, whether it be sadness or sincerity, Ian couldn't be sure. He would take Levi at his word. For now.

An hour later, the kids' mini-bull riding clinic was well underway. Between the fathers, the professional bull riders, the volunteers like Levi, and the rodeo clowns, enough people were in the arena that someone had been assigned to Ian to keep him protected while he joined them in the dirt.

For the first time since he'd been following the rodeo, he could photograph from inside the arena, and with the bulls being not much taller than a Great Dane, his chances of serious injury were minimal.

He got far enough away that he could lay in the dirt and take his shots of the kids in their tiny hats and chaps and toothy grins. Then as he stood and changed rolls of film, his focus shifted from the riding, and he found himself taking other shots. He hadn't realized what he'd done until he'd almost finished another thirty-six-shot roll that didn't have one bull in it.

Ian aimed and photographed the little six-year-old on his father's shoulders, the father's large hands gripping the miniature boots. The man's over-sized cowboy hat on his son's head dipping down in front of the boy's eyes. The peal of infectious laughter ripped a scar deep inside Ian's chest, a pain, a hollowness. For a fraction of a second, Ian wondered if one of the bulls had gotten lose and gored him.

Might have hurt less than watching what he'd never had.

Knowing that there might have been a man out there who could have given that to him, ate at his gut. For the first time since he'd heard about his mother's infidelity, the anger and resentment grew at the fact that his mother had kept his *real* father from him.

Perhaps a good, loving one like the man in front of him.

Even before he'd learned that Patrick Murphy wasn't biologically his father, Ian had long since given up trying to please the bastard. Climbing Mt. Everest in shorts and flip-flops would have been easier.

But Ian couldn't let loose the idea that maybe, just maybe, he would have made his *real* father proud.

He would have appreciated the opportunity to try.

Feeling a hand on his back, he turned to find Cora beside him.

"Everything okay?" she asked.

He swiped at his eye. "Dust is bad out here." He led her to the side of the arena, out of the fray so they could talk without having to worry about getting trampled.

Cora leaned against the wall and eyed him. She hadn't swallowed the lie. "Dust, huh?"

He cleaned off his lens. Just because he didn't like how easily she read him didn't mean he wanted to lie straight to her face, so he didn't say anything.

She tugged on his camera strap to get his attention. "Have you thought anymore about trying to find out who your father is?"

Hooking up with the rodeo was never supposed to be about him, but he'd learned more about himself in the last few weeks than he had in the last twenty-four years of his life. As difficult as it could be sometimes, he appreciated that Cora didn't fear asking the hard questions.

He blew a stubborn spec of dirt off the lens and replaced the cover. "Where would I even start? There had to have been four million men running around New York when I was conceived. Any one of them could be my father."

"You said your step-father didn't know who your real father was, but were there any other family members that your mother might have confided in? That would be a hard secret for your mother to keep to herself all those years. Surely, she would have told someone. A sister, a cousin, a friend?"

The hint of a smile curled his lips, and Ian ducked his head and went in for a kiss. "You're a brilliant woman, Cora Hayes."

He grabbed her hand and pulled her out of the arena. She laughed that full laugh that went straight to his heart and said, "Where are we going?"

"The rodeo office. I've got a phone call to make."

It took some wheedling and a touch of his Irish brogue to sweet talk the rodeo secretary into allowing Ian to make a long-distance call on the fairground's phone.

After the older woman left the cluttered office to give him and Cora some privacy, Cora said to Ian, "You're a menace with that accent. Whipping it out when it suits, leaving little old ladies powerless to resist your bidding."

He waggled his brows and gave her a cheesy grin. "I gotta use what I can. No one wants me to bat my lashes or shake my ass to get what I want."

Cora stepped in close, looped a finger through one of his belt loops, and grinned up at him. "I don't know about that."

The open invitation in her eyes almost had him reaching for the lock on the door and taking her right there against the rodeo secretary's desk. One of the things he loved about Cora was the fact that she probably wouldn't be opposed to the idea.

Loved?

Loved *about* her. Not *love*-love *her*.

Right?

Ian leaned against the desk and picked up the phone. The initial excitement of calling his aunt and maybe finding out who his real father was, faded as he stared into Cora's sky-blue eyes. God, how much he'd miss her when he was gone. While in many ways he was still the outsider in this rodeo crowd, he'd already begun to feel like he belonged here with Cora.

A dangerous way to think.

The telephone operator looked up his aunt's number and connected the call. As the phone rang and rang, his chest got tight, his heart thudded, and blood swooshed in his ears almost as intense as if he'd just come back from a run. Except that a run didn't leave you feeling unsure and vulnerable. On a run, your world wouldn't crumble with your next step.

His insecurity, and his inclination to end the call must have shown in his eyes because Cora stopped pacing. Somehow, she knew how much this phone call meant to him. More than he'd been willing to admit to himself.

She said, "Let it ring."

He rubbed the back of his neck, but he let it ring and ring. Soon the secretary would want her office back. Ian started to lower the receiver when he heard his aunt's voice.

He closed his eyes and tried to swallow past the sudden stricture in his throat. Aunt Eileen sounded bold and brash...she sounded just like his mother had.

Clearing his throat, he said, "It's me. It's Ian."

Silence. Then he heard her breathing. Or maybe that was him.

For a second, he thought he'd have to identify himself some other way but then his aunt said, "How's me wee laddie?"

He chuckled. "It's been a long time since I could be considered little." But considering his father had only taken him to see her once since his mother had died, he couldn't fault her.

"Your Da told me—"

"He's not me Da," he bit out. *Jesus*. Get a fucking grip. "Sorry. I'm not angry with you."

"Don't be too hard on the man. He loved ye mum, he did. In his own way."

"Yeah? He had a damn funny way of showing it."

The conversation had just started, and he already felt drained. Ian sunk into the chair and motioned for Cora to come over. When she did, he guided her to his lap, craving the contact, the closeness. She settled against his chest, one hand massaging the back of his head.

"Ian…It was a different time. He was raising another man's ba—"

"Bastard. You can say it, Aunt Eileen."

"*Baby*. I was gonna say baby, lad."

Maybe. "Yeah. Sure." Clicks and pops and static came over the line as his aunt waited for him to speak again. This wasn't a call to catch up. It was a call for answers. "Do you have a name? For my real father?"

More static, then a sigh. Heavy. Sad. "No. A photographer he was. For the Times. That's all ye Ma would tell me."

It had been a long shot. One he hadn't known was so important to him until he felt the sting at the back of his eyes. He blinked a couple times. He would be hard pressed to blame his watery eyes on wind-swept dust while they were in an office.

"Did Ma tell him he had a son?"

"He never knew."

Ian didn't know if that made him feel better or worse. At least he knew that his real father didn't outright reject him. The man didn't even know he existed.

The rodeo secretary stuck her head in the door and Ian held a finger up, letting her know he was almost finished. "Look, I have to go. Thank you."

"Come see me sometime, lad."

"Sure," he said, though he had no intentions of returning to New York anytime soon. If ever.

———

Cora tacked Panache up for the barrel race, more than a little annoyed. She hadn't had more than five minutes alone all day and three of those minutes had been when she'd disappeared into the women's restroom. Even then, Ian had waited outside. If the crowd hadn't been so heavy that night, he probably would have followed her in if it wouldn't have gotten him arrested.

Now, Scottie Hines sat on her tack locker in front of her stall, chewing on a piece of Panache's hay.

"I know you need to be getting some of the stock ready to move. You don't have to babysit me. There are plenty of people in the barn. I'm not even close to being alone."

"Josephine asked me to wait with you until she got back from taking her horse to see the rodeo vet. So that's what I intend ta do."

Cora blew out a frustrated breath, and Panache reached around and lipped her arm when she pulled on the cinch too hard. She loosened the leather strap and patted her horse on the neck. "Sorry, boy." Then to Scottie said, "I think this has been blown all out of proportion. There's been no direct threat. Just some idiot trying to scare me or mess up my runs."

"Can't never be too careful."

"Yeah? Well, I'm about to tell a certain city slicker where he can shove his—"

Scottie cleared his throat and nodded his head toward a spot over her shoulder. "Murphy."

Cora glanced over as Scottie gathered up his can of Skoal and slipped by Ian. Ian clapped him on the back. "Thanks, man."

Scottie didn't answer, he just tipped his hat as he walked down the aisle toward the indoor chutes and the herd of bawling cattle.

"Talkative fellow. Where's Josephine?" A hint of accusation crept into his voice. "She was supposed to be with you until your race started."

Cora gave him the side eye, then had Panache lower his head so she could put his bridle on. "This is a rodeo, not Fort Knox. It's not like you need to post a guard on me twenty-four/seven."

He glared back. They'd been through this more than once today. Ian refused to back down, and while their friends had closed ranks and offered to be with her during the times Ian couldn't, Cora knew he would soon find out that their friends had more important things to do than babysit. They all had their own lives to lead that didn't involve her and her issue with some crazy-ass secret admirer.

He moved in close and took her hand. "Look at me." She wanted to refuse, but the concern in his voice had her meeting his eyes. "You're more precious than a room stacked with gold. If I could put you under lock and key, I'd do it in a heartbeat if I knew it would keep you safe."

"But you can't."

"Unfortunately."

He wrapped an arm around her waist and removed her hat long enough to press a kiss to her forehead. Panache turned his head and nudged his front pocket searching for treats. Ian scrubbed his hand through Panache's thick, cream-colored fore-lock. "I've got nothing, boy."

Panache blew out a heavy sigh, his large nostrils flapped, sending a shower of horsey snot in all directions. "Ewh." Cora backed away and found a towel to wipe her hands on. "He knows how to spoil the mood."

Then she reached into her back pocket and pulled out a piece of paper. Her heart did a crazy flop and her stomach folded in on itself at the thought of handing the list over. She didn't know if what she'd done was the right thing to do, but she'd had to find a way to help. Hopefully, Ian would see it that way as well.

He'd been quiet since the call to his aunt. He'd told her the basics, that his aunt didn't have a name. That his real father didn't know about him, and that he'd been a photographer for the *New York Times*. Would Ian think she was meddling? That it wasn't any of her business?

"What's that?" he asked.

After a moment's hesitation, she handed over the list she'd obtained. "It's a list of photographers the *New York Times* employed around the year you would have been conceived."

He glanced from her face to the paper and back again. He wasn't smiling. In fact, he took a step back and regarded the paper as if she held a bomb. Then again, in some way that list could have the ability to blow up his life. What the hell had she been thinking?

"Um...I..." Before she could take the paper back, he took it from her hand, but instead of opening it, he stuffed it in his pocket. He had this expression on his face that she couldn't quite read. "I should have asked before I called the *Times* and asked for the names. I just thought...you know..."

Ian hitched a thumb over his shoulder. "Don't you need to warm him up?"

Here she was dressed for the arena in her cowgirl shirt with the sparkles, her best jeans, chaps, hat and her horse freshly brushed and saddled with her race the farthest thing from her mind. Even though he'd been deflecting, Ian was right. Time to focus.

She took Panache's reins and started down the aisle. She turned to Ian and said, "You don't have to come if you don't want. There are plenty of people around the warm up arena and Josephine should be back any minute."

"I'm coming." Though he didn't look happy about it. Or maybe he just wasn't happy with her.

On the way to the warm up arena, he trailed a couple horse lengths behind her and Panache. She tried to shift her attention from him to her job ahead. Josephine had loaned her a few bucks that morning, and if Cora didn't win a check tonight, she wasn't sure what she was going to do for money.

She swung into the saddle, and she and Panache walked into the arena. After a few trips along the rail, she lost herself in the gentle rocking of Panache's canter, of the hollow drum of hooves in the dirt, on the buzz of conversations punctuated by laughter.

Taking a deep breath, she rolled her shoulders, letting the tension fall away. She forgot about the stupid secret admirer and about her man who'd been wronged.

Yes. *Her* man.

Even if he was only hers for now.

12

After a night at the local bar celebrating Cora and Panache's win, Ian, Cora, and Josephine pulled into the parking lot at the Santa Fe rodeo grounds. Being the good friend that she was, Josephine drove Ian's truck, with Cora smashed between Josephine and Ian. With her winnings, Cora and Ian had gotten more than a little drunk. Now Ian looked forward to climbing into a warm bed and passing out for the night.

Ian grabbed his hat off the dash and climbed out of the truck to walk Josephine to her trailer. In the glow of the headlights, Ian glanced back through the windshield. Cora's eyes lay at half-mast as the alcohol and the stress and the excitement began to drag her under. Ian glanced back at the trailer and drew up short.

Cora must have noticed because she hauled herself out of the truck using the steering wheel and the open door for balance. "What's wrong?"

From where she stood, she couldn't see the step of the trailer, but Ian bent and picked up another dead rose and newspaper clipping.

Josephine glanced over at Cora, Josephine's face pale in the shine from the headlights. "Who the hell is doing this?"

"I don't know," Ian said. "But if I get my hands on the bastard, he's going to wish he hadn't."

Cora stepped between Josephine and Ian. "Let me see."

Ian wanted to hide the clipping from Cora, it would only scare her more, but Cora wasn't the type of woman to run from her problems. She was the type of woman who faced them head on.

"More of the same," he said. "Only worse. I don't know what you did to piss this person off, but this is getting worse not better."

Cora stared down at the dead rose. Instead of just the clipped picture from the newspaper of her dancing on the table at The Wheel, someone had taken the time to cut around the picture of Cora and pasted it on a sheet of paper. At the top it said, "I only have eyes for you."

"I guess this means we can rule out a jealous barrel racer," Josephine said.

"And rule in a jealous lover?" Ian added. He tried to keep his voice level, but a hint of accusation must have slipped out because Cora and Josephine both slid him a look that hit like a one-two punch.

Speaking of jealous lovers... Ian leveled his gaze at Cora. "You never did give me that list of boyfriends."

Her chin went up. "This mean I get a list of all the girls you've had sex with?"

"That isn't what this is about, you know that." Ian fisted his hands on his hips.

Josephine took a step back, her hands raised. "I'm going to bed. You two can slug this out."

"Were not fighting." Ian and Cora said at the same time.

Josephine unlocked the trailer door, a small smile playing at the corner of her mouth. Despite the seriousness of the situation, she directed her comment to Cora, "Sure you're not. Who's the jealous lover now?"

Cora huffed out a breath as Josephine disappeared inside the trailer. "I'm not jealous."

Ian glanced up and met her eye, man enough to admit what he was feeling, even if he didn't want to feel it. "I sure as hell am."

Josephine stuck her head outside the trailer door. "You guys care to take this somewhere else? A girl's gotta get her beauty sleep."

"Yeah," Ian said. "Let's get out of here."

"Presumptuous of you to assume I'm staying with you tonight."

He took a moment to count backwards from three. "Cora," he said dropping his voice and taking a step toward her. "Let's not do this."

"Fine." The word came low and throaty like a growl. Ian took Cora's elbow, grabbed his keys from his ignition, and led her to his trailer.

Ian followed her in, sitting across from her at the kitchen table. Reaching beside him into the small drawer of the kitchen cabinet, he pulled out a pen and a pad of paper and slid it over to her. "We need a list. This isn't about who you slept with. This is about finding out who is a threat. This isn't going away."

"Maybe he's just trying to get attention." Cora looked hopeful, but not *too* hopeful.

"He's got our attention. If we ignore this, if we ignore him, what's to keep this lunatic from going after Panache, or you?"

Cora uncapped the pen, and started doodling in the corner of the pad, short, slashing, hard lines that dug into the paper. "I just want all this to go away."

Ian reached across the table and took her hand; her fingers cool to the touch. "Me, too, baby. Me, too."

While Cora worked on her list, Ian gave her some space and prepared his entry for mailing the next day. When he'd finished, she still hadn't completed the list, so he started going through some of his negatives to find other photos he'd promised some of the riders he'd print.

Word had gotten out, and he was doing enough of a side business selling prints to the rodeo crowd to keep him in grub and gas if nothing else.

Finally, she put the pen down, and rested her chin on her bent knee. "That's it, I think."

Ian was almost afraid to look. The list had taken a while, but it wasn't like she'd been scribbling the whole time and having to use two or three or four sheets of paper. Instead, she'd been thoughtful and methodical. Ian had little doubt that whoever was responsible would be on that list.

Reaching across, he spun the pad around and read through the names. "This all of them?"

"All of the ones who have been with the circuit since this nonsense started, but not all of them, no." It came out as a challenge. As if she dared him to take exception.

As if she expected the admission to scare him off.

If that had been her intent, she'd have to try a hell of a lot harder than that, because besides the occasional flashes of misplaced jealousy, he found the way that she owned her sexual history with bravado and not shame, tripped his ticket. He reached a hand down and adjusted himself.

Together they went down the list one by one, ranking them in order of what Cora termed the *creep factor.*

Trouble was, many of the men Ian had already met and, good or bad, the reality was the majority of them seemed like decent men. Good, that it might be easy to narrow the list. Bad, because it was frightening to think that one of the 'nice' ones could be responsible. The man at the top? Levi Banks.

"Why's Levi at the top?" Ian had gotten to know Levi a bit better over the past few weeks, even considered him a friend.

"Only because he was the last guy I was with, and because of the whole pregnancy thing with him. He's ready to settle down. The whole wife and kids waiting for him back home. I'm nowhere close. I know he wants kids. That's part of the reason I knew we wouldn't work out. At least not in the long run."

"How'd he take the break-up?"

"Harder than I'd expected."

Which, to Ian, explained the whole way Levi hadn't been able to keep his eyes off Cora that first night back at The Wheel.

"But he's with Patty Bennet now. It's not like I ruined him for women forever."

Maybe. Patty or no Patty, Cora hadn't seen the way Levi had watched her. The torch Levi still carried for Cora hadn't been extinguished. Not by a long shot.

"How do you want to handle this?" Ian asked. Cora wasn't the type of woman who waited around for a man to fix her problems—which he admired—unless it came to sexing her way to winning a barrel race—in which case he couldn't complain.

"We start at the top and work our way down, asking questions."

"They could lie. Most likely will lie, whoever it is."

Cora said, "Short of catching this guy leaving the roses and clippings or finding a stash of dead flowers and a stack of newspapers from the *El Paso Tribune,* we'll have to hope a little bit of pressure will make him confess."

"Or in the very least back off."

"I could live with that." Cora spun the notepad around and around, deep in thought. Then her expression shifted from contemplative to concern. "Did I mess up earlier? Getting that list of photographers from the *Times*? I wasn't trying to pry."

In the back of his mind, his father's—scratch that, Patrick's words— came back to Ian, where he'd called Ian's real father a pussy. As bad as Ian had had it growing up, and despite all of Patrick's faults, at least Patrick had been there.

"I know. I'd just come to terms with the idea that my real father is out there, somewhere. The thought that I could actually find him is surreal. What do I do, get a list of phone numbers, call up a bunch of strangers and ask them if they fucked my mother?"

Cora's expression went neutral, except for the fact that her brows nearly met her hairline.

Ian scrubbed his hands over his face. "Sorry about that. I'm not mad at you. That nerve's a little raw.

"Don't be sorry. You have a right to be angry, Ian."

Ian chewed on her words. Cora was right. He had a right to be angry at his mother, at Patrick and his aunt for keeping the truth from him, for making his life up to that point feel like a total lie.

"Did you recognize any names on the list I made?" Cora asked.

"A few. Guys who'd moved on from newspaper work and got some notoriety in the bigger magazines like *Rolling Stone*, *National Geographic*, and *GlobeTrotter*. Guys I could probably get in contact with through the magazines. But there are names on that list that I wouldn't even know where to begin looking to find the guys, unless they're still in New York and are listed in the phone book. Thought I could get my aunt to look up some people that way."

"I noticed Edward Lark is on that list. Your idol. Maybe when you win the contest and get to travel with him, you'll get a chance to ask him face to face if he's your father."

Ian barked out a laugh. "As amazingly awkward and freakishly groovy as that would be, Lark is old enough to be my grandfather, not my father.

"At least now you know you came by your love of photography honestly."

"Maybe that's why my mother bought me my first camera and encouraged me along the way."

"Maybe it wasn't your mother who bought you the camera," Cora said. "Maybe your real father bought it for you. Maybe that's why Patrick was so opposed."

Ian's gaze went to the two open shelves above his kitchen counter, where he stored spices and whatnot. On the top shelf, in the corner, sat his first camera, the one his mother had given him. Could it be true? Could that camera have come from his father? "Maybe, but remember my aunt said he never knew about me."

"Wouldn't be the first time someone in your family lied to you."

Ian had to laugh at that. Depressing as the thought was. "Touché."

Cora toed out of her boots and socks and scrunched down in her seat, resting her feet on the seat beside him. He placed them in his lap and took her feet into his hands, pressing his thumbs into her insteps.

Her head fell back, and her eyes drifted closed. "Mmm...that's almost better than sex."

"Then I must be doing something wrong."

"I did say 'almost.'" She got a lazy, sexy grin on her face. "But I'm not opposed to some sex. Strictly as a direct comparison."

The deep throated moan the extra pressure he placed on the balls of her feet elicited made the dregs of his anger fade and his arousal intensify. "Challenge accepted."

IN THE SATED AFTERMATH OF SEX THE NIGHT BEFORE, IAN HAD

taken advantage of Cora and managed to extract a promise from her not to confront any of the men on her list without him. He'd been careful not to make the same promise.

The long haul over to Oklahoma meant he'd had plenty of time behind the wheel to think about what he'd wanted to say to Levi, but no opportunity to do so. Until now.

Ian had left Cora with Josephine as the women took advantage of an enclosed barn and a wash rack with hot water to bathe their horses and put on a spit shine for their runs later that night.

Cora might not appreciate him going behind her back, but with Levi becoming more of a friend, Ian had felt this was one talk he needed to tackle man to man.

Ian walked into the local bar down the street from the Oklahoma City rodeo grounds, the bar where the rodeo crowd had taken over for the weekend.

Mid-day on a Friday, there wasn't a whole lot of drinking going on. More like eating, shooting pool, shooting the shit, or catching up on some much needed zzz's in an out-of-the-way corner. Tables had been moved to the side and guys were laid out haphazardly on the mostly clean floor, their hats over their faces, the tops of their boots under their heads while they slept to keep their boots from being stolen.

Pulling the cap from his lens, Ian made adjustments for low light and snapped a couple of pictures of the sleeping men, trying to find inspiration for a follow-up story should he be lucky enough to be one of the finalists.

Too bad, none had come.

That's because you already found your story.

Ian shook his head. No. He wasn't going there. Those other photos he'd taken of Cora, striking as they were, had been for him and for her. No one else. He'd *promised* her.

Though that didn't keep him from wishing things were

different.

Pushing his work to the back of his mind, Ian made his way through the bar to a front booth by one of the windows.

"Can we talk?" Ian asked Levi as he slid into the seat across from his friend.

Levi was busy applying conditioner to a pair of chaps, the scent of leather and oil heavy in the air. Levi bobbed his head—not to Ian's question—but to the low beat of the country music coming from the jukebox near a couple of what looked like local rednecks playing pool.

"Why do I think this isn't a social call?" Levi stopped rubbing the oil into the leather long enough to give Ian a wary eye.

"I could buy you a beer." Maybe if Ian got Levi lubricated enough, he wouldn't take offense at the question he needed to ask.

"I've gotta ride tonight. What's on your mind?"

Okay, so no lubrication. As laid back as Levi came across, Ian couldn't forget that the man wrestled steers for a living. That, and Ian had seen the man hold his own while out-numbered in a bar fight.

"I'm going to ask you straight. Are you the one leaving the roses and clippings for Cora?"

Levi's face remained placid, but the dead-eyed glare he shot Ian could have stopped a charging bull. Ian was glad there was a table between him and Levi, though the man was big enough, strong enough, fast enough to come over the top of it before Ian would be able to do anything to stop him.

"Come again?" Levi's words came out like a dare.

"You were the last one to be with her. I don't think it's a secret you still have unresolved feelings. I could understand if there was some hostility there, her breaking it off with you and all." Ian skirted that fine line. The one where he might be able to get Levi mad enough to say something in the heat of the moment and maybe give himself away, and the one where Ian got himself killed.

With the number of rodeo guys in the bar, if shit went south, it didn't matter how good of a fighter Ian was, he'd lose. Teeth for sure, if he were lucky, maybe a kidney or two if he weren't.

"I'm with Patty now."

"That's doesn't answer the question."

Levi refused to break eye contact. So did Ian.

"There a problem?" One of a circuit guys from a few tables over asked Levi. A bronc rider if Ian remembered right.

"Give us a minute," Levi said to the man, though his focus never wavered from Ian.

The man grumbled but got up and left. Ian broke eye contact long enough to glance around. There wasn't another person within earshot. If Levi wanted privacy, this would be about as good as it got.

"Cora's a great woman," Levi allowed.

"I can see why you'd still want her, even if she's moved on."

With measured care, Levi placed the cap on the leather conditioner and set it and the rag aside, not to be neat, Ian decided, but to give Levi time to be precise with his words. "I'm not the guy you're looking for."

"But you still have feelings for her."

Some of the anger left Levi's eyes, allowing some of the hurt to flood in. Would that be how Ian was going to look when it came time to say goodbye to Cora?

Ian's stomach twisted, knowing at this point that he was already in so deep with Cora, it would be less painful losing a body part.

The barest, briefest, of nods was all Levi allowed, before he said, "But I don't want to hurt her. I don't know what I can do to convince you of that. You have my word. That will have to do."

"You could let me see your camper. Let me see you don't

have dead roses and extra newspapers."

Levi's eyes flashed, and Ian prepared to block a punch.

"I could also tell you to fuck off."

"Or you could humor a friend who's doing what he can to keep Cora safe."

Levi leaned back, and a caustic laugh clawed its way past his throat as he grabbed for his chaps and cleaning supplies. "All right, asshole. Let's go."

———

On Sunday night, Cora and Panache continued their winning streak. Not first place, but in the money, which Cora would gladly take to the bank. Again and again and again.

Instead of hitting the bar with Josephine, Levi and the rest of the rodeo crowd for a celebratory drink, she followed Ian to the bank of pay phones by the rodeo office to place the awaited call to *GlobeTrotter Magazine* to see if the contest results had come in.

With a stack of coins and a number written on a scrap of paper, Ian made the long-distance call and waited with his foot tapping while it rang.

"Hello?" Ian said into the receiver. "This is Ian Murphy. Entry number twenty-three. I'm calling to see if the contest results are in." He paused. "Yes. I'll wait."

They waited. And waited. In the distance, a truck pulled up and disgorged a load of people that laughed and giggled and staggered back to their trailers. He wrapped an arm around her shoulder, drawing her in. She cuddled up against him, soaking up his warmth.

Tension coiled in his body and his heart beat a rapid staccato beneath his ribs, a sharp contrast to the facade of calm he posted on the exterior.

Like her, Ian internalized a lot, not wanting anyone, even her, to know how much this meant to him. Cora heard the tinny voice as the operator came on and at her prompt, Ian deposited more quarters. He pressed a kiss to the side of Cora head. "They're killing me," Ian muttered in her ear, talking about the interminable wait.

Cora gave him a squeeze of encouragement. At least with barrel racing, the only thing she had to beat was the timer. A win was concrete. Indisputable. Not subject to the fickle opinions of another person.

If it were up to Cora, Ian would win, hands down, and she wasn't just saying that because she warmed his bed at night and had firsthand knowledge of his physical creativity.

As amazing and phenomenal as the sex was, the depth of emotion, the sheer provocativeness that he'd created with his camera, with his mind, was unadulterated genius.

Ian stiffened, and held her tighter. "I'm still here," he said into the phone.

A series of 'Uh, huh's' and 'I understands' and head nods came next, his expression never changing as he took the information in. "You're sure," he said at last. "There's no mistake?" He pinched the bridge of his nose. "No. Yeah, I get it. Okay."

Cora's heart dropped in her chest, the weight heavy against her diaphragm. He missed the cut. She couldn't breathe.

As bad as she felt for Ian, there was this teeny, tiny horrible piece of her that was secretly glad because if he didn't win, then maybe he'd stick around.

This isn't his world, Cora. You can't use sex as an erotic carrot to hold him hostage.

"Thank you," Ian said at last, hanging up the phone. He pulled her against his chest as he leaned back against the wall of the rodeo office. He scrubbed a hand over his face, his fingers scraping against the scruff on his jaw. He sighed. "I don't believe it."

"They're idiots." Cora knew firsthand how much it sucked to lose. Maybe the judges weren't idiots, maybe everyone else's entries were just as good, just as moving, or even more so than Ian's, but honestly, she couldn't see how. Then again, all she knew was how his work had made her feel.

"I'm a finalist."

"Wait." Cora took a half step back. Did he say what she thought he'd said? "You won?"

Ian gave a little shrug, a smile of disbelief finally curving his lips. "Not won. I made it past the first round."

"Same thing," Cora said.

"Hardly." Ian caught her when she jumped into his arms and planted a big wet kiss on his lips. "But I'm one step closer."

She locked her heels behind him. Pinning her hands behind his neck, she pulled back enough to see his face. "You're not nearly as excited as I'd thought you'd be. What's wrong?"

He set her down. "They moved the deadline up. Finalists were supposed to have a week to submit their final entry, but the editors decided to put the contest winner in the next issue. So, if I don't send my next photo essay out first thing in the morning, it won't make the new judging deadline."

"Don't just stand there," Cora said, "You've got work to do."

"It can wait," Ian said.

With that tight of a deadline, Cora knew it couldn't. Catching the nutjob throwing a wrench into her life couldn't come fast enough. Having a babysitter twenty-four seven got old...fast. "You go do what you have to do. Josephine should be back from the bar soon, and she and I can go ahead and pack up and get ready to head out for Shreveport in the morning."

"I don't—" Ian cut himself off, the conflict clear on his face— in the jump of the muscle at the corner of his jaw, the tension around his eyes, the taut muscles in his body as if what he needed to do, and what he wanted to do, warred within him. "This is fucked up."

"No. It is what it is." Cora took his hand and pulled him away from the wall and started dragging him back toward his camper. He'd gone above and beyond, supporting her in her dream. Now it was her time to return the favor. "I'll wait at your trailer until Josephine comes back. Packing can wait. Your project can't."

Linking fingers, they walked back to Ian's camper. A truck pulled in, its headlights raking across the gravel parking lot with that distinctive chug-chug-cough that could only be Josephine's truck. They detoured to Cora's trailer and met Josephine there. She climbed out, a big cheesy, half-sauced smile on her face. Good thing the bar was within walking distance and she hadn't driven far.

"Tag, you're it," Cora said. "Ian has some work that can't wait."

As Josephine closed her truck door and took a staggering step, Ian leaned in and whispered in Cora's ear. "I don't like this. She's going to be more of a hindrance than a help if anything happens."

"It's been more than a week since the last note, and we've cleared more than half the names on the list as best we could, maybe this guy has given up, or changed his mind."

The grip Ian had on her hand tightened. "Or, he's waiting for us to let down our guard."

Cora bit back the flash of annoyance and the inclination to roll her eyes. All this super heightened alert left her physically on edge and emotionally drained. "I'll pump her full of instant coffee. That should wake her up enough to kick ass if she needs to."

Josephine toddled over and patted Ian on the chest. "Go on, lover boy." The slurring was minimal, but obvious. "Us girls have got this."

13

Cora and Josephine walked back to the stalls after packing their saddles, bridles, and saddle pads into the back of the trailer and started gathering the extra buckets, grooming supplies and whatnot, and loading them into their portable tack lockers.

The half-drunk, half-caffeinated thing wasn't working in favor of Josephine's mood. Josephine grumbled, "We forgot to get the dolly."

Cora glanced at the tack lockers. With a total lack of enthusiasm, she said, "We could each grab an end."

"We still need to haul the hay bales back. Might as well go get it."

Up ahead, Scottie Hines turned down the aisle with a handful of gauze squares and a bottle of disinfectant. "Evening, ladies."

"What's up?" Cora bobbed her head toward the armful of medical supplies.

"One of the steers tore a chunk of hide off his flank on something. I was going to clean it up a bit, make sure we don't need to call the vet in and get stitches. The rest of the crew are still at the bar. I could use a hand if you have a minute."

"You go," Josephine said to Cora. "I'll hunt down the dolly."

Josephine must have realized what she'd said because then she added, "Wait. I'll go with you. Ian wouldn't want—"

"It's fine." Cora rolled her eyes. Ian wasn't her father, and even if he were, everyone knew how little she listened to the preacher. Besides, Ian might be her self-appointed protector, but Cora wasn't some damsel in distress. She was fully capable of protecting herself. Besides, she'd be with Scottie. He wasn't as big and imposing as Ian or Levi, but Josephine wasn't exactly Muhammad Ali either.

Since his hands were full, Scottie bumped his chin towards a series of indoor pens. "We'll just be over there."

Cora started walking backward toward the pens, not giving Josephine the option of stopping her. "I'll be back in a few."

Near the steer pens, Scottie turned on a bank of lights, and they searched through one pen and then the other looking for the injured steer. "It's one of the black ones."

"These all look fine," Cora said.

"Yeah, damn it. I told Forney and Thomas not to turn him out with the others, but they must have forgotten. He's gotta be out back in the overflow pens."

Behind the main and warm up arenas were a series of outdoor pens, used to catch the overflow from the barn. With all the roping steers, bulls, and bronc stock, there was never enough room inside the barn.

"Thanks anyway," Scottie said. "I'll have one of the guys help me in the morning."

"We're here. We have the supplies. Let's do it now. I'd hate to see it get infected."

"You sure? It's kinda cold out. We could go back to your stall, get your coat—"

No way would she give Josephine the chance to talk Cora out of helping. "I'll be fine. It's not like we're going to be out there forever."

Scottie gave her a tobacco-stained grin. "Thanks. It's not like he's one of the prize bulls, but Olivia is a stickler with her stock, she'd tan my hide when I got back to Texas if the animals weren't in good shape."

Outside, the air had a bite as they made their way down the aisle between the pens, the pole lights bright enough to see where they were going, but they were going to have a tough time finding a wound on a black steer in the generally poor light. Luckily, they only had one pen of steers to search.

"I'm going to hop in the pen," Scottie said. "You run around to the other side and get ready to open the gate. I'll herd him through and we can run him up to the squeeze chute."

Cora went around, the smell of urine and manure strong as she manipulated the gates. It took a little doing, but Scottie soon found the injured steer and managed to cut it from the herd, the other calves scrambling and mooing, their breaths coming out in white puffy clouds.

The calf ran through the gate and Cora slammed the gate closed behind it and shooed the animal through the chute. Scottie dropped down behind the steer, waving his hat to encourage it to move forward. As it ran through the squeeze chute, Cora pulled the head-gate lever, catching the calf behind the head, trapping it.

The calf bawled, slinging slobber and rolling its eyes. It kicked at the rails as Scottie jumped over to her side and added pressure with the squeeze panel to keep the steer still enough for them to work on it.

With the animal immobilized, they quickly determined that no stitches would be required. In a matter of minutes, they had the wound cleaned, the salve applied, and the steer turned back in with the herd.

Cora closed the last gate and turned, running smack into to Scottie's chest. "Oh, sorry," she said as she stepped to go around.

Scottie shifted, putting his hand on the rail beside her head, blocking her in a tight corner. She hadn't noticed until now that he hadn't brought the medical supplies back with him. When she looked up, Scottie had a dark enigmatic expression on his face. Her skin pricked, and her hands fisted on their own.

But this was Scottie.

This was her friend.

She forced her hands to relax, but met his eye when she said, "I need to get back. Ian will worry if—"

Scottie scoffed and, that close, Cora smelled the liquor on his breath for the first time. Her hands fisted again.

"What are you doing with him anyway?" Scottie asked, his voice a weird mixture of pleading and misplaced concern. "He's not what you need."

"That's not up to you to—"

He leaned in close and whispered in her ear. "We have a connection, Cora. Can't you feel it?"

"What are you talking about?"

He palmed her cheek. "This. Us."

She pushed his hand away. "There is no 'this'. No 'us'."

"Baby, baby…don't be like that. Murphy is the first guy you've been with since the winter circuit started. We both know that's because of what we shared. Everything you've confided. What we mean to each other goes beyond sex, it's—"

"It's all in your head." The cold statement brought Scottie up short. He tilted his head like a puppy who couldn't understand basic commands. Cora's core went deathly cold, and a shiver skittered up her spine and buried in her brain.

"No. Last season you were with a lot of men." He took a step closer and she took a half of one back before the rails of the corral stopped her retreat. "But that's okay, baby. I don't blame you or hold it against you. But this season was different. We talked. We connected. Things changed. *You* changed. For a while, you stopped sleeping around—"

Cora pressed a hand against his chest. "Stop." His heart thumped beneath her hand, while hers beat triple time, the roar of blood past her eardrums made even her own words sound far away. She decided to go with the truth and end this little delusion before Scottie ran away with it. "I didn't stop sleeping with men because you were in my life. I stopped sleeping with men because of my pregnancy scare."

"That's not true." His words came out soft, with a note of hurt. Cora might have felt sorry for him if he hadn't wrapped his hand around her wrist, his grip just shy of bruising.

This was getting out of hand.

Getting?

Okay, was already *way* out of hand. Cora stood straighter, getting on her tippy-toes to get in his face. "You need to back the fuck off."

Yanking her hand, she tried to pull free, but Scottie proved stronger than he looked. Far off, Ian called her name. She heard the tension in his voice, the rising fear, the near panic of not being able to find her.

She opened her mouth to scream, but Scottie pressed up against her, his mouth covering hers, swallowing her screams as he forced his tongue into her mouth. The taste of stale tobacco and cheap liquor churned her stomach and made her gag. His leg came between her thighs, his body pressing her back until she was shoved into the rails.

Tearing her face away, she dragged in a quick breath, but his hand came down over her mouth before she could yell out. If Ian was still calling her name, he'd gone in the other direction because she couldn't hear him any longer, and what little sounds she could make were easily covered by the bawling of cattle and the neighs of horses.

"You going to be quiet?" Scottie asked.

She nodded her lie. "It's you, isn't it?"

The realization settled in with the truth of her words. It had been Scottie all along who had sent her the clippings and the roses. That he hadn't even been on her list should have left her feeling cold and vulnerable, instead it made her blood boil as the adrenaline spiked in her system.

"If you just let it, we could be so good together. You don't need him." Scottie said the words like he was a reasonable man, like she would turn to him and say, 'yeah, you're right.'

When she wanted to fight, when she wanted to run, she had to force herself to keep her wits about her. With his body pinning her, she couldn't kick or knee or punch with any effectiveness. To fight him, her advantage wouldn't come from her size and muscle, but from her wits.

"Why didn't you tell me how you felt?" Cora said, biding her time until she could catch him off guard. The hand she'd laid on his chest, didn't push him away, instead, she slipped it around the back of his neck and pulled him closer. "Can you forgive me? For being with Ian, for not—"

"Oh, baby." Scottie eased closer and rested his forehead on hers. "We all make mistakes."

He took a step back to look at her face. Cora worked hard turning her sneer into a smile. She could hear Ian calling again, as well as Josephine, still far away. Out in the far, dark corner of the stock yard between the pens and several outbuildings, she and Scottie wouldn't be easily spotted.

Sliding her hands down Scottie's arms, she gripped his hands and he let her pull them from her shoulders. She had to get back to the barn, back to where Ian or Josephine had a chance of helping her. "Then let's go tell Ian," she said. "You and me."

She looked him directly in the eye as he rubbed his thumbs across her palms. Biting the inside of her cheek, she suppressed a shudder, and hoped the poor shadows would help disguise her insincerity.

"You mean that, don't you, baby."

She stood on tiptoes and pressed a kiss to the day-old scruff on his cheek. With a certainty she didn't feel, she said, "I do."

She took a step back, pulling him with her toward the barn, the tension coiling in her belly, every nerve, every fiber of her being telling her to fight, telling her to run. But she stood a much better chance of getting away if she could get him back to the barn voluntarily. She didn't have to fake her sincerity when she said, "Come on. We can end this now."

She took a step, then another, her hand sweaty in his despite the chill outside. His grip tightened, and he yanked her back until she banged into his chest. "You didn't really think I'd fall for that, did you? How stupid do you think I am?"

"Ian!" She yelled at the same time she wrenched her arm back, jerked her hand free, and sprinted toward the barn.

Scottie tackled her from behind, slamming her into the hard-packed dirt. Her head bounced, rattling her brain in her skull. Lights dimmed, her vision blurred then cleared as they rolled and grappled on the ground. She tried to call out, but most of the breath had been knocked out of her, she'd been lucky she hadn't passed out.

Scrambling to his feet, he grabbed both of her wrists and started dragging her toward one of the outbuildings. Cora kicked a foot out, catching a corner of one of the pens, the sudden halt jarred one hand free. She twisted. She rolled. She hollered out loud, but the fight had stirred all the animals and their moos and neighs and running hooves made it hard for her to hear anything.

Was Ian even coming?

For a split second, she broke free, her boots sliding in the dirt as she fought for purchase. Scottie grabbed her around the waist, but she managed to elbow him in the ribs. He grunted, his grip loosening enough for her to struggle to her feet. She took advantage of the moment, taking the heel of her hand and smashing it into his nose.

Scottie howled, his hands going to his face as blood flowed between his fingers. "You bitch. I should have known you were no different than the rest."

Her reply came as a swift kick to his nuts. Scottie must have seen it coming because he pivoted at the last second. The glancing blow knocked him to his knees, but as soon as he hit the ground, he fought his way to his feet.

Cora only had seconds before he went after her again. With him blocking the way back to the barn, she couldn't chance him catching her as she tried to run by him. She did the only thing she could—and ran the other way.

She sprinted down the aisle and squeezed between the rails of the back fence and kept running. Past the outbuildings, past the empty field at the back of the rodeo grounds, with any chance of help getting farther and farther away. Behind her, came the slap of Scottie's boots and the ragged hitch of his breath as he bolted after her.

The muscles in her thighs burned and her heart raced as she called out for help. For Ian. For anybody. The deserted back alleys offered no protection. She cut down a side street and headed toward the main drag with the bars and hopefully some people.

If she could stay ahead of him.

She wasn't the fastest runner, especially in boots. Scottie

gained some ground, but adrenaline fueled her flight. Up ahead, the street lights got brighter, and a car pulled out of a parking lot, its headlights raking across her body.

Waving her arms, she called out. The car never slowed. It turned and accelerated down the road, with Scottie only a few steps behind her. Then she broke out onto the street and wrapped her hand around the post of a stop sign to help her with an abrupt change of direction, catching Scottie off guard.

His momentum took him into the street, but she made the turn and sprinted down the sidewalk, headed for a set of neon lights that simply said, 'Bar and Grill'. The desperate move helped her gain a few feet of separation, but she knew it would be fleeting.

Her chest heaved, huge gasping breaths—the entrance to bar twenty feet away. Fifteen. As much as she wanted to glance over her shoulder, she couldn't spare the time. Every step, every breath, every heartbeat, she expected to feel his hand on her shoulder.

Ten more feet.

She caught movement out of the corner of her eye. Before it could register in her brain, the blow came to her ribcage as Scottie tackled her to the ground. Cora's head slammed against the pavement. Pain radiated around her skull, a blinding, searing pain that had her curling into the fetal position, her hands over her head, unable to defend herself as the stars in her vision faded and went to black.

After pouring over a bunch of negatives, and having chosen the best shots to enlarge, Ian pulled the last of the prints out of the rinse bath and hung them in the shower to dry. While he waited, he opened his windows to air out the camper and packed away the tubs of developer and fixer.

He looked out the front window, looking for Cora, but someone had moved their stock trailer into his line of sight and he could no longer keep an eye on their trailer while he packed. He glanced at his watch. Just after midnight. Cora should be done by now, but he knew how she and Josephine could sometimes get sidetracked and get more talking than packing done. He wasn't worried. Not yet.

Instead of starting to gather all the loose items laying around on the table and counters in preparation for heading out in the morning, Ian stood in the bathroom doorway, his arms crossed, his back resting against the jamb as he glanced over the glossy eight-by-tens.

He waited for the pang of guilt to hit. None came. Even though he'd promised Cora, when it had come down to the story he wanted to tell, there was none more important than the one in his heart, the one that starred a tough, hardworking, courageous woman who wasn't afraid to live her life on her own terms.

If after he showed her the story, if she refused to give her consent to use the photos he'd taken of her on her journey from the struggles of trying to make a life for herself on the circuit to the joys of having her hard work pay off, he'd just wouldn't have a new entry for *The GlobeTrotter*. No point in sending in anything other than his best work, even if that meant he wouldn't win.

For the first time since he'd heard about the contest, since he'd had the dream of escaping overseas and hunting down stories, of sharing lives and hardships and triumphs from around the world, his determination faltered.

Because for the first time in his life he *had* a life and wasn't just going through the motions. He had friends he liked, he had work he enjoyed. More importantly, he had a woman that he loved.

For once, leaving his old life behind had fallen off the top of his priority list.

He glanced at his watch again. If she didn't return in five more minutes, he'd go hunt her down, even though he knew it would piss her off.

His gaze went from picture to picture to picture. *Wait.* He stiffened. All of them were of Cora, but it was the background that caught his attention and made the hair on the back of his neck rise, and the blood prick like jagged ice through his veins.

Of the ten photos, seven of them had Scottie Hines in the distance. Not of him in passing, or working, or generally minding his own business, but of him standing in the background, his focus on Cora.

"Son of a bitch." Ian tore out of the camper, heading straight for Cora and Josephine's trailer. As he rounded the stock trailer, he saw Josephine hauling a bale of hay to her trailer, he glanced behind her but there was no sign of Cora.

He skidded to a stop in front of her. "Where is she?"

"The barn. Why?" Josephine dropped the dolly and followed Ian as he jogged toward the barn. "Ian, what's wrong?"

"You weren't supposed to leave her alone."

The barn seemed miles away when, in reality, it couldn't have been more than seventy yards. But when every step you took felt heavy and monumentally slow, it might as well have been.

Along the way, he tried to tell himself he was wrong, that Cora was fine, and he didn't have anything to worry about, but the violent roll of his stomach told him otherwise.

"I didn't. She went to help Scottie with a wounded steer," Josephine said, her words came out harsh as she panted trying to keep up with his pace.

That roll his stomach was on did a couple of nauseating loops and spins like some sort of nightmare roller coaster. "I think it's Hines," Ian said, not having the time to explain what he'd seen. By the look on Josephine's face that was all she needed.

"Cora!" Ian called out as he broke into the barn. He stopped long enough to listen for a response. Nothing. Only the scuff of a couple of hooves and a few half-asleep horse heads popping up above the stalls.

"They said they were going to be by the big indoor pen."

Ian called out again as he ran for the pen and the bank of barn lights. He slapped the big vapor light on for the entire barn, his eyes slowly adjusting as the lights gradually came on. Ian ran down one side of the pen and Josephine ran down the other.

"I don't see them anywhere," Josephine said.

"Go hunt down one of the security guards, tell him I'm headed out to the stockyard."

He didn't wait for an answer as he called out for Cora again and beat it toward the overflow pens, looking both ways down all the aisles as he ran, making sure he didn't miss her along the way. Even though he ran most every day, his breath became ragged, his chest constricting as his fear rose. This was all his fault. He shouldn't have left her alone with Josephine to pack, no matter that Cora had insisted.

Then he heard it. His name. "Cora!" Somewhere, somehow, he found another gear, his legs churning through the dirt and dust.

He burst out of the back of the bright barn, into the poorly lit stockyard. He stopped, not knowing which way to go. With the animals riled up, he had a hard time hearing any cries for help.

Then he heard her scream. Adrenaline dumped into his

system burning white and hot, narrowing his focus. At the far end of the stockyard, he saw the movement, the scuffle.

He didn't think, he just ran, knowing if he didn't hurry he could lose them in the streets. "Hines!" Ian hadn't expected the man to stop, if that was him, but the word ripped from his throat, jagged and cutting.

He ran like his life depended on it because it did. Nothing mattered except catching Hines. Not who his real father was, not his contest entry, not even his burgeoning ambivalence with winning.

Only Cora mattered.

Reaching the spot where he'd last seen Cora, Ian hopped the fence. No one was in sight. He stopped, listening for Cora calling out, or for the slap of boots on pavement, but all he heard was the deafening roar of the blood past his eardrums. A rushing, gushing sound as if he were drowning.

Emotion swamped him—fear, guilt, anger, denial. Thinking about what more he could have done to protect Cora to find the man responsible. Ian fought through the emotional onslaught, focusing on finding Cora.

He made a split-second decision and ran toward town, instead of through the field to the trees beyond. With Hines on Cora's heels, her best chance was heading towards people.

Running, running, running, Ian took the most direct route to the main drag. The flat soles of his leather boots slid on the concrete as he stopped at the street corner. Watching, listening. On the outskirts of town this late at night, traffic vacillated between sparse and nonexistent. At least until the bars closed for the night. She screamed, and he spun. He caught a flash of movement disappearing into the alley beside the Bar and Grill. He took off again, arms pumping, feet pounding.

As he raced towards Cora, he knew one thing for certain...

Hell was not this mythical, infernal place of fire and brimstone and eternal damnation that clergy always preached about.

Hell was real.

Hell was here and now.

Hell was terrifying, soul-wrenching. Hell was knowing the woman he loved was in mortal danger...and he may not be able to save her.

Up ahead, the Bar and Grill's door opened, spilling out a man and woman along with laughter and a steady country twang. Ian recognized Levi from the shape of his hat and the formidable build.

Ian pointed and hollered, "The alley. Cora."

For a big man, Levi proved fast on his feet, taking off for the alley at a dead run, beating Ian by good ten seconds.

Ten of the longest, most agonizing seconds of Ian's life.

Taking the corner at top speed, Ian miscalculated his trajectory, slipping and slamming into the side of the building, the pummeling his shoulder took hardly registering. What did register was Cora's still form sprawled across the alley, Levi pressing Hines against the wall, Levi's fist landing blow after brutal blow to Hine's gut and face.

That Levi might kill Hines was a fleeting thought. But seeing Cora on the ground made it hard for Ian to give five flying fucks.

"Cora." Ian fell on his knees beside her, the dark, dank scent of piss and rancid garbage hung in the air, too heavy for the mild breeze to dissipate.

Levi and Hines scuffled behind him. Was Cora even breathing? "Talk to me, baby." He reached a hand out to check her pulse, terrified of what he'd find. Beneath a shaking hand, he found the steady thrum of her pulse.

Alive. She was alive.

Elation, and relief, mixed with a cauldron of dark emotions hit Ian until he didn't know what or how he felt. He only knew that this day would go down as singularly the worst and best day of his life.

A crowd from the bar started gathering at the head of the alley. "Call an ambulance," Ian said as he took her hand and gently patted her cheek. "Wake up, baby. It's okay. You're okay. Just come back to me."

"And the police," Levi called out.

Ian spared a glance at Levi. The bulldogger had Hines' face pressed against the brick wall, one arm to the back of the slime bag's neck, the other pinning Hines' arms behind his back.

He brought his focus back to Cora, at the stillness of her form, at the scrape at her temple, at the tear in her shirt exposing her bra.

Vengeance reared its head, a cold, savage beast. He stood, slow and deliberate, not a blinding rage, but a calculated retribution. Sirens wailed in the distance as Ian stalked over to Hines.

"I've got him," Levi said.

A restrained Hines didn't mean this all ended. "Now it's my turn."

Ian grabbed the back of Hines' collar and scruffed him like a mangy kitten. Hines grunted.

"Back off," Levi said, "you don't want to do this."

"There's nothing I want more." Ian pushed Levi away. Levi must have recognized the murderous intent in Ian's eyes, because the big man raised his hands, not wanting any part of a pissed off Ian.

Ian spun Hines around, and Hines' head bobbed on his shoulders, smacking against the brick with a hollow sound that Ian felt more than heard. Blood dripped from what look like a well-broken nose, and Hines' eyes threatened to roll back into his head—at least the one eye that hadn't almost swollen closed already. "You slimy sonofabitch."

Shaking him again, Hines didn't put up any fight, his arms hanging limply at his sides, his knees buckling. If Ian hadn't had a tight grip on Hines' shirt, the man might have crumpled to his knees. That didn't keep Ian's fist from forming or his arm from rearing back. At the last second, Levi caught Ian's arm, spoiling a punishing punch.

"I told you to back off," Ian spit out. He considered Levi a friend, but if he had to go through Levi to get to Hines, he would. The grip Levi had on Ian's arm tightened. "She's awake."

"Ian, no." Cora's voice came out scratchy and weak.

How Ian heard her over the sirens and the storm of footfalls as the sheriff's deputies and paramedics flowed into the alley, he'd never know.

He locked eyes with her, Hines momentarily forgotten. He shoved Hines away, and Levi must've caught the man because Ian never heard a thud.

Pushing past the deputies, Ian knelt beside Cora as she struggled to sit up.

"Easy," a paramedic said. "I want to make sure nothing's broken."

"I'm okay, I'm okay." Cora swayed, and Ian caught her, bracing his weight behind her.

"You don't seem okay. Be a good girl and let this guy check you out."

When Cora cut him a look at the 'good girl' comment, Ian knew no permanent damage had been done.

A hint of a smile curved her lips. "You're gonna to pay for that remark, buddy."

Ian cupped her face and pressed his forehead to hers "I look forward to it."

14

The paramedics checked Cora out. A deputy got her statement. Somewhere in all the confusion, Scottie's sorry, stinking, betraying ass got hauled off to jail. Cora had no idea how much time had passed, only that it was late, and the rodeo grounds were dead quiet.

As Ian gingerly handed her up into his camper, Cora knew there were a lot of things she should be feeling, wired being the least of them.

"You ready for bed?" Ian asked, his eyes bloodshot from lack of sleep.

"No," she said. "But you go ahead. You look beat."

Ian's eyes softened at the word 'beat' and he reached out, cupping both of her cheeks. He pressed a brutally gentle kiss to her split lip. She sank into him and he held her there in the middle of his camper, as he pressed kiss after kiss to the side of her head, to her neck, her shoulder. Not as if he wanted to get it on, but as if he needed the constant reassurance that she'd survived relatively unscathed, besides the mild headache, a few bumps and bruises, and a scrape at her temple that the paramedics had cleaned and bandaged.

Scottie hadn't fared as well. Last she'd heard, the deputies had to detour to the hospital on their way to taking him to jail.

Physically, she'd heal in no time. Emotionally, she felt drained, but on edge. The reality of what happened would certainly hit at some point. Mentally, she prepared herself for that time to come, but right now, she needed not to think about it.

"Come sit with me," he said as he took a step back and held out his hand. She appreciated the way he stuck by her, supported her. Not just in the save her ass kind of way she still needed to thank him for, but with his emotional support.

Ian wasn't the kind of guy that got off telling her 'I told you so'. He'd be the one to say, 'we'll deal with this together.'

She'd miss this when it came time for him to leave.

Taking his hand, she said, "I don't deserve you."

"That's where you're wrong. I think we both deserve exactly what we have and what we've built." His features softened, and he got a look on his face as if he wanted to say more.

"What?" she asked.

"I..." Then he gave her a sad, contemplative smile as if he couldn't be sure what he'd wanted to say would be something she wanted to hear. "Never mind. You've had a shit day. It's nothing that can't wait."

Standing in the confines of the camper, the stench from the alley on her clothes made her eyes water and his nose wrinkle.

"Why don't you let me help you get cleaned up," he said. "I promise to behave myself."

Cora looked at the man she'd approached for a friendly fuck because she thought he was safe, only to find out the sexy, compassionate, protective, creative man in front of her, the man she was falling hard for, had the ability to destroy her. Even knowing that, she couldn't help slapping her hand on the destruct button. "I can't promise the same."

Ian took a step back, pointing a warning finger in her direction. "Behave. Now strip off those clothes while I get the shower running."

By the time Cora had undressed and stuffed her dirty, stinky clothes into a garbage bag for a trip to the laundromat later, Ian had removed the photos he'd had drying in the shower and put his enlarger away.

"You still have your clothes on," Cora said as Ian ushered her into his pill box of a shower.

"There's no way the two of us will fit. Relax and let me do all the work."

As much as she'd like a naked Ian in the shower with her, the idea of his soapy hands roaming all over her body completely turned her on. "If you insist."

The hot water tank on the camper wouldn't last long, so after wetting her down with the detachable shower head, he lathered up his hands and shut the water off. Coral leaned against the back wall and closed her eyes.

The hot water he'd sprayed on her skin quickly cooled, and goosebumps ran down her body from the tops of her shoulders to the tips of her toes. His hands started with hers and worked their way up her arms to her shoulders, then down her torso. The long, sensuous strokes had her head lolling back and her knees threatening to give.

He left no inch untouched, her breasts, her buttocks, and more, until it took all her will power not to drag him in with her, clothes and all.

"If you are trying to get me to relax," she said, "you're doing a piss-poor job. All I want to do is touch you. You need to get naked."

Ian chuckled, the deep rumble making her shiver as he turned the hot water back on and rinsed her body. She wanted him, needed him, but when she reached out, he gently batted her hand away.

"This is about doing for you," he said, "not the other way around. Lean back so I can wash your hair without getting your bandage wet."

Her grumble quickly turned to a groan as he worked his fingers into her scalp. "You know, if this whole photography gig doesn't work out for you, you could totally pimp yourself out as a wet masseuse."

He threw his head back and laughed. Considering the night they'd had, it was a good sound to hear. "Is that even a thing?"

"If not, it should be."

"I'll keep that in mind," Ian said as he finished rinsing her hair and shut the water off.

He wrung out her hair and wrapped her in a towel, leaving her to get dressed while he got himself cleaned up. He came out in nothing but a towel. Her hands went to the flap he'd tucked into the roll of terrycloth around his waist.

"You need to stop," he said.

Cora's hand stilled, one wrist flick away from getting everything she wanted. "I thought you liked—"

His hands were warm when he took hers. "I like. Plenty. I just think that maybe sex isn't what you need right now."

"Shouldn't that be my decision?"

Reaching around her, he snagged a pair of sweatpants off the bed and slid them on before removing the towel.

"You're not going to answer me?" Cora asked.

"I want to put this in a way you'll understand."

"I got a scrape on my head, not brain damage."

Ian held up his hands. "That's not what I meant."

Before she could get too pissed off and back away, he leaned against the counter and pulled her between his spread legs, his arms wrapped loosely around her hips.

"You need to wipe that look off your face," she said.

"What look is that?"

"The one where you look like the parent about to teach a life lesson to their kid."

Ian schooled his face. Though Cora debated if she liked Ian's new and improved look. "If you were at a bar, and Josephine was too drunk to drive, what would you do?"

"Take her keys."

"What if she insisted that she was fine. That she *wanted* to drive. Would you let her?"

Cora knew where Ian was going with this. "I'm not drunk."

"But you may not be thinking clearly."

That he could maybe have a point, kept Cora from arguing, even if she didn't entirely agree.

Ian kissed the tip of her nose. "As your lover and your friend, this is me taking your libido keys." Then he grinned, that sexy, goofy grin that made her stomach light and her heart do somersaults in her chest. She was *so* gone with this guy. "But only for the night. If you want to bang like bunnies in the morning, I'm all for it. I promise."

She reached down and cupped him and gave him a nice firm stroke through his sweats. Despite his words, his body responded, ready to mutiny. "You may regret that promise."

For a moment, his eyes fluttered closed and he bit back a groan, then his grin broke into a full-fledged smile that lit his eyes and transformed his face. "Doubt it."

———

Giving Cora's ass a dismissive pat, Ian said, "Go have a seat. I'll make us a couple of hot chocolates."

Cora settled in at the camper's kitchen table, dressed for bed in the Mets shirt he'd lent her the first night, and a pair of cut-off sweatpants. She'd ripped the neck out of the T-shirt and it hung off one shoulder, the swell of her breasts pressing against the thin fabric, making his dick impossibly hard.

Even though he knew he'd done the right thing turning her down, it hadn't made doing it any easier, not when every second of every day he wanted her more and more.

The pan of milk on the stove bubbled. He killed the gas and stirred cocoa powder and sugar into a couple of coffee mugs.

He set the mugs down and settled across the table from her. One by one, she went through the set of photographs he'd left on the table. The story to accompany his entry still needed writing. Considering what had happened that night, he found the motivation to do so difficult to find.

That, and he had to find a way to convince her to let him use the photos he'd taken of her. It seemed like a dick move to ask her now, after Hines' assault.

Taking a sip of the hot chocolate, she glanced up at him. "This is for your final entry." Not a question, nor an accusation.

He offered no excuse. "Yes."

In the quiet, her eyes got misty. He'd expected to see hurt, or anger, or hell, even a sense of betrayal, but he couldn't read her expression or her silence.

In his defense, he added, "I know we had a deal. I respect that. I'd planned on asking you before I sent it in." Now he started to prattle, his nerves egging him on. "Trust me, I don't want what happened before to happen—"

"This is your only entry." Again, a certainty, not an inquiry.

As much as he wanted to win that contest, the cost of losing her to achieve his goals wasn't a price he could pay, even if their relationship had an expiration date. He blew out a breath and nodded. "It is."

He waited for the backlash.

Waited some more.

She patted the seat beside her and he warily scooted around the table, taking up the corner spot in the wraparound booth. "Which ones would you use?"

He'd expected a lot of questions. He hadn't expected that one. Was she seriously considering giving him her permission? Moving the mugs out of the way, he flipped through the photographs and laid four out on the table in order, the ones showing her transformation from her lowest low to her highest high.

Cora brought her leg up and rested her chin on her knee looking from one to the other to the other. Ian's heart raced, waiting for her response. Not as terrified as he'd been seeing her unmoving form in a dark alley, but scary just the same. Having someone see his work, see into his heart when they saw what he saw, took getting used to. At the same time, it left him feeling raw and exposed and vulnerable, and strangely proud.

"Wow." The word came out breathless. Cora swiped at her eye.

Oh, shit. He hadn't meant to make her cry. "Baby, if it upsets you, I don't have to use them."

"But you don't have anything else you can use for the contest."

"Fuck the contest. It doesn't matter."

"It does to you."

Ian hitched a finger under her chin. "Not as much as you do."

"You mean that, don't you?" Her cheeks pinked, and her laugh hitched as she dried her eyes with the heels of her hands.

"I wouldn't have said it if I didn't."

She sniffed, then flipped back through the stack and added another photo. "I think this should be in there, too."

He glanced at the additional photo she'd chosen. The one they'd taken together on the beach. The one of her with her lips on his cheek. There was a tenderness there, a sweetness that combined with the other photos said that while you fight for your goals, you can't forget to live your life. "Yeah?"

She smiled wider as her eyes dried. "Yeah."

"I like that even better."

The photos had all been cropped close on her face. Running the gamut from desperation, to hope, to determination, to realization, and finally to triumph. A story anyone who has struggled could identify with.

"I've seen these looks on other people. This isn't just my story, it's everyone's story." Cora had to clear her throat. "Everyone struggles. Everyone has to overcome."

The statement the photo array made, had his throat constricted and his chest tight, the emotion swelling against the surface. That she got that and supported him, made her acceptance even more special.

"I think the universal message is 'you are not alone,'" she said.

The weight on Ian's chest eased. One hurdle down, one more to go. A moth buzzed and batted its wings against the plastic shield around the kitchen light. Outside, all was quiet, deep in the night. "You know if I win, this is getting published. Not only in the United States, but around the world. Are your parents going to approve?"

She reached over and linked her fingers with his. "I don't know. Probably not. Even though the photos aren't racy or scandalous. These past weeks I've learned some things about myself. The most important one is that I can't live my life to try to please my parents."

"I came to that same conclusion the hard way."

"I'm an adult. I don't need their permission or approval or blessing. This is me. They can take me or leave me."

Then she scooted out of the booth and dug his typewriter

from beneath the seat of the other booth and set it on the table. He scooted around and took his place in front of it, his grin making his cheeks hurt.

With a hand on the seat back, she leaned in, placing her other hand mid-thigh. His dick stirred as she planted a kiss on his lips, her face serious when she said, "Thank you for finding me tonight."

His throat closed at the thought of what might have happened to her if he hadn't found her in time. It would take a whole tub of grease to slick his words up enough to squeak past the stricture, so he nodded in answer.

Then that familiar glint lit her eyes as she went in for a longer, deeper kiss, her hand sliding up his thigh and stroking the erection tenting his sweats. She pulled back. "Work fast. It's almost morning, and you promised me we'd fuck like bunnies."

———

THE NEXT SATURDAY NIGHT AFTER A QUALIFYING RUN, AT THE Austin County fairgrounds, Cora dug out the change she and Ian had scraped together in preparation for his call to *Globe-Trotter Magazine.*

They waited as the minutes ticked by, waiting for the clock to strike midnight, the time the magazine had said the winner would be announced. Four more agonizing minutes. Carefully, she lined up the quarters, dimes, and nickels, biggest to smallest, on top of the metal box around the pay phone.

"Your hands are shaking," Ian said as he captured them in his and tried to rub the cold away.

A cold front had come through, and for South Texas, the normally mild winter had turned frigid. She curled into him, letting his body block her from the wind. Only problem was, the blowing wind and the freezing temperature weren't responsible for the shaking.

As the clock on the outer wall of the rodeo office moved one minute closer to midnight, her apprehension ratcheted up. Three short minutes and she'd find out if Ian had won, and if he would have to leave the circuit.

Leave *her*.

This casual thing with Ian had turned serious, her heart in way too deep. The confliction she felt warred inside her, knotting and twisting her guts until even liquids felt like they'd come right back up. As much as she wanted him to win, she selfishly wanted him to lose.

"You ready?" Ian said as he lifted the receiver and picked up a coin.

She shoved a smile out onto her face, a little too big, a little too bright to be real. "Sure."

His fingers worked the dial, going through the numbers as she called them out. When he reached the last one, she watched the dial rotate back into place, the tiny tic-tic-tics of the dial sounding loud and electrified. Ian put his arm around her shoulder and held the receiver between them both.

She shook him off. As immature as it may be, she couldn't bear to hear the news. "This is your moment. I don't want you to miss a word of it."

He pressed a kiss to the side of her head, right above her ear. She could hear the inhale of his breath as he breathed her in. Then he whispered in her ear. "Love you."

What?

Cora opened her mouth. Nothing came out. Then into the phone Ian gave his name and entry number. "I'm calling for the contest results. Are they in yet?"

Love you. Love you. Love you.

Ian's words echoed in her brain. Had he realized he'd said

them? They hadn't said those words to each other before. To her, saying 'I love you' seemed like a commitment to the future, one that was so high up in the air, Neil Armstrong would have to strap a rocket to his ass and orbit the earth to see it.

Ian squeezed her shoulder tighter and Cora tuned back in.

"...and you're positive there's no mistake?" His voice went higher, and Cora heard the suppressed excitement in his voice as if he were afraid to believe the truth. "When—*What?*"

Ian made a writing motion with his hand and Cora pulled a Bic pen off the nearby bulletin board and handed it to him. He scribbled something on his hand, reading the numbers back to make sure he'd gotten them correct.

"Um...No, sir," Ian said, "That won't be a problem. Thank you, sir."

Ian hung up the phone and ran his hands through his hair. Cora couldn't help the smile even though at the same time, the pain she felt deep in her chest had to be her heart breaking. "You won."

Ian shook his head, disbelieving the news at the same time an infectious grin spread across his face. As much as she didn't want him to leave, she was also thrilled for him. He'd done it. His chance to make his mark on the world lay at his fingertips.

"I won," he said, the incredulity clear in the words. "I actually won."

"I'm so proud of you." Cora wrapped her arms around his waist.

He held her tight as the moment sunk in, then he threw his head back and laughed, swinging her around. "I won!"

Setting her back down, he cupped her face and planted a smacking kiss on her lips. "Thank you for letting me use those photos, if it hadn't been for you—"

She placed a finger to his lips, shutting him up. "That was

your heart, your vision in those photographs. The world deserves to see your inspirational work."

Only one thing needed to be settled. Cora feared asking the next question, but not knowing would be worse. She rested her hand on his chest and asked, "So how many weeks do we have left before you have to go?"

Ian's smile slipped and turned stark. He stepped back and ran his hands down his face. Cora stepped toward him. "Days?"

Slowly, he shook his head and swallowed hard. "Hours," he managed.

Hours. "No. I—" She motioned between the two of them. "We—" Her voice broke and her throat constricted. She couldn't have said anything even if her brain could wrap its neurons around what Ian had told her, which they couldn't. She'd always known this would end, she hadn't expected it to be *now.*

"It's sudden, I know. It wasn't supposed to be like this, but things have heated up in Vietnam and Lark is catching an Army transport plane out of New York first thing Monday morning. If I want to go on assignment with him, I have to catch the first plane to New York I can get."

This was really happening. Cora didn't know if it was the cold or the wind or the pain in her chest, but all the oxygen in Texas seemed to have vanished. Sucking in a deep breath didn't seem to help.

Pull your big cowgirl boots on and deal now, cry later.

"Don't cry." He brushed a tear off her cheek.

Damn. Damn. Damn. She could do this. "They're happy tears," she lied. "We'd better call the airlines and get you a ticket."

———

"You all packed?" Cora asked as she entered Ian's trailer after taking care of Panache for the morning.

Ian rubbed at his gritty eyes and waved a hand at the duffel bag and camera equipment piled on and around the kitchen table. "I think I've got everything."

Ian had hardly slept the night before, making sure he had all his bases covered. He'd lined Levi up into taking his truck and camper to a nearby storage facility the next day. At least his flight to New York would get him back home in time to grab a few necessities before he had to meet Lark and catch the overseas flight.

"You sure you don't need a ride to the airport? I could—"

Ian cupped her shoulders with both hands. "We've been through this. I'm fine with taking a cab." He checked his watch. "In fact, it's scheduled to pick me up in two hours. I don't want you missing your run and missing out on a possible check because of me."

Which wasn't true at all. He wanted her to take him to the airport and to spend every last second they had left together, but he wasn't selfish enough to stomp all over her dream to accomplish his.

"Two hours? Your flight isn't until later tonight."

"With the rain and the freezing temperatures coming, I didn't want to be on the road if things got icy."

She took that in, and he watched her shift through her emotions. The disappointment. The sadness. Then she nodded, more to herself than to him, and he knew from her beautiful, benevolent, breathtaking smile that she'd dug deep to make the most of the time they did have left.

She waggled her brows at him and reached for his belt. "Two hours, huh? There's a lot we can do in two hours."

A part of him wanted to spend the two hours talking, but as

she undid his jeans and slid them off his hips, he wouldn't miss the chance to make love to her one last time before he left.

Blood rushed south as she dropped to her knees in front of him taking him in her hand and then her hot, wet mouth. "Jesus Christ," he ground out, the words guttural and gruff.

He tugged her ponytail holder free and fisted his hands in her hair, holding and guiding her as she went down on him, her tongue tracing along the underside of him up to the ridge, around the head. Light, teasing strokes that had his spine tingling and his balls tightening.

He pulled back, and she glanced up at him. "Something wrong?"

Cora's hand replaced her mouth and the easy strokes and the way her thumb brushed across the tip of his cock made forming a complete thought almost impossible. He helped her to her feet, kicking off his boots and jeans.

He stroked a hand down her cheek, his thumb brushing against her bottom lip. "If this is our last time, I want to be inside you when I come."

Leaning in, she kissed his neck, his jaw, the spot below his ear and whispered, "Have your people call my people and we can see what we can arr—"

Her squeal of laughter cut through the air as Ian grabbed her up and tossed her onto his bed. He shucked the rest of his clothes and got rid of hers. Reaching for a condom he slipped it on and climbed into the bed.

His arms shook as he held his weight on them and he reached down between her legs. Hot. Wet. Ready.

"I really wanted to take this slow, but—"

"Shut up and fuck me already," Cora said.

He grinned down at her. He loved the way she didn't fear saying what she wanted. Loved her take it or leave it attitude.

Except with the way she'd wormed her way into his heart, he

had no option but to take it. Take her. Again and again, as long as she allowed.

He filled her in one long, balls deep stroke.

"Mhmm," Cora purred as she grabbed his ass and sank him farther. "I'm going to miss this."

As much as it killed Ian to think about her with other men, the reality was they might never see each other again. She had her life to live and that didn't include waiting around for when, or if, he'd come back stateside.

If this assignment went well it could be a long time before he returned, so he kept his tone teasing and light when he said, "I'm sure you can find someone else more than willing to help you keep winning checks."

She stilled beneath him. Her smile disappeared, and a line formed between her brows. "That's not what this is." To emphasize *this*, she ground her pelvis against his. He bit back the groan. "It hasn't been about that for a very long time. I'm with you because I want to be. Not because I have to be. You know that, right?"

He nodded once. In his heart he'd known that. His head had taken a little longer to catch up.

Cupping his cheek, she raised up against him, long, luxurious strokes, that made her eyes dilate and breath catch. "I...I—"

He cut her off with a kiss, wishing the L word sat on her tongue, knowing it would gut him to hear yet again that she didn't want a relationship. He broke the kiss. "I know. You don't have to say it."

"I just—"

"Babe. Don't over think this."

The line between her brows eased and a smile teased and toyed with her lips. "What are you trying to say?"

"What you so eloquently said to me before...Shut up and

fuck me already."

Cora laughed that boisterous laugh he'd come to love so well. "Gladly."

He rose up on his knees, her ankles locking behind his thighs as he drove into her over and over again. She met each stroke as he ran a hand down her abdomen, the muscles fluttering beneath his touch.

Palming a breast, he brushed his thumb across the peaked nipple. His breath came quick and sweat slicked his skin as their bodies slapped against each other. The rhythm rapid, rushed.

Bracing his weight on his hands on the bed beside her, he ducked his head and took her nipples into his mouth one after the other, her skin slightly salty. The moan he elicited from her had him pumping harder.

"I'm close," she huffed out, her cries of pleasure driving him on.

"Touch yourself." He leaned back on his haunches, taking hold of her hips and watching her as she slid a hand down her body, her fingers dipping into her folds and circling her clit.

Once. Twice.

Quite the sight to see as his dick pounded into her.

Then her head fell back as her body stiffened and her muscles clamped down around him, milking him and sending him over the cliff. He caught his weight on his arms, and slowed the pace, drawing every last tingle, every last sensation out.

"Mmmm...That feels so good," Cora moaned as she caressed his ass.

"Never better."

Still half-hard, he didn't want to stop, but he pulled out and took care of the condom and grabbed another, just in case. They rolled onto their sides, and he pulled her back against his chest, their bodies fitting together, her ass to his cock.

He pressed kisses against her shoulder while his hand

roamed over her body, not to excite, but to feel, and to memorize her softness, her warmth.

"I'm going to miss this," she said.

'Me, too' perched on his lips. Only a half truth. He'd miss making love with her, but not only that, he'd miss her and the fun they'd had together. The way they shared their lives, their failures, their successes. He didn't want to leave her with just that. He wanted to leave her with the full truth.

Into her ear, he whispered, "I love you Cora Hayes. If I could stay—"

"Shhh." She laid her hand over the one he had splayed across her abdomen and directed his hand between her thighs. "Again," was all she said.

Retrieving the other condom, he put it on and he eased in from behind, taking it slow this time, knowing this memory might have to last a lifetime.

15

———

Don't cry, don't cry, don't cry.

The cabbie blew his horn for Ian, and Cora went to sit up.

"Stay there," Ian said. He opened the trailer door long enough to hold up a hand to let the cab driver know he'd be a minute. Then he came back and sat on the edge of the bed where Cora lay tucked beneath his covers.

He rubbed a hand on her shoulder. "You've got the address I gave you for the unit we'll be embedded with?"

"I do."

"I don't know how well the mail system works over there, but I'll write when I can and send them to Josephine's father's ranch. Since your father doesn't approve, I don't know how else to get letters to you. You're never in the same place for more than a weekend."

"We can only do what we can." Cora forced the optimism into her voice, no way was she sending Ian away with tears. That's not how she wanted him to remember her.

But damn...it hurt, and those tears would fall, but at least he wouldn't be there to witness them.

Ian cleared his throat. "Do you regret it?"

It. Them.

Her throat spasmed. Before it completely closed up, she managed. "Not for a second."

He smiled down at her, sad, proud. "That's my girl."

Outside, the horn honked again. Cora tried to get up, but Ian's gentle hand on her shoulder held her down. "I want to walk you out."

He brushed the hair out of her face. "Stay." Pressing a kiss to her lips he added, "I want to remember you here in my bed."

Cora choked on a laugh. "Fair enough."

Again, the horn.

"I gotta go." He laid a lingering kiss on her forehead, his thumb brushing her cheek.

Going to the table, he shouldered his bags and opened the door. Looking back one last time, his smile somber when he said, "Stay safe, and in case I never get to see you again—" His voice cracked. When he spoke again, it came out soft. "Have a good life, Cora Hayes."

Then he stepped through the door.

Gone.

Cora lay in his bed, surrounded by his scent, by the smell of the sex they'd shared and waited for the tears to flow. Somehow, they didn't fall, even though the searing pain in the middle of her chest where her heart used to be felt like one of the bulls had used her for target practice.

All she wanted was to stay and wallow, but as she glanced at the clock above his kitchen table, she knew she had to rush if she were to get showered, dressed, and have Panache tacked up in time for their run.

She could wallow all she wanted later.

A couple hours later, Cora and Panache waited near the alley for their chance to run. For a Sunday night, the rodeo crowd in the bleachers was light. The bad weather with the threat of sleet and possibly snow kept many of the fair-weather Texas fans tucked away in their warm houses where they could catch the action on television.

Josephine and Comet trotted over after spending time in the warm-up arena. From head to toe, Josephine had decked herself out in her riding best. From her hat to her sparkly shirt, to the shine on her new boots. Even under the harsh lights beneath the stands, Comet's coat shined, his thick muscles flexing and contracting with each step.

"You don't look so good." Josephine said when she pulled Comet to a stop beside her.

Panache and Comet nuzzled noses. They were as close of friends as she and Josephine were.

Cora huffed a laugh. "That's a couple steps up from the way I feel." Then her eyes got watery, and she swiped at her cheeks, a streak of black mascara coming off with her finger. Why couldn't she have cried before she had her makeup on? "Jesus, what a mess."

Josephine handed her a red bandanna. "Keep it. I have a feeling you might be needing it."

Cora dabbed at her eyes. "He told me he loved me."

"Good thing he left then, I know you never wanted—" Josephine cut herself off. Cora couldn't keep the pain and heartache off her face. She'd thought if she told herself that his leaving was for the best, that she hadn't been looking for anything serious, all those things meant to bury the truth and the hurt, that those lies would make his leaving easier.

Guess what? It didn't.

"Holy, shiiiit," Josephine said, drawing the word out as the realization struck. "You love him, too."

Cora nodded. The announcer called a number and a barrel racer trotted by them on their way to the arena.

"He left, even knowing—"

"I didn't tell him."

"Are you *freaking* kidding me?" Josephine cried out. Heads turned. Josephine either didn't notice or didn't care. She also didn't lower her voice. "You may never see this guy again, and you let him leave without knowing how you felt?"

"He said he knew. Said I didn't have to say it." The excuse sounded weaker out loud than it had in her head. "He has his own dreams, his own plans. I didn't want to screw that up."

"Have you thought that maybe if you had given him a reason to want to change his plans, that he might have?"

Cora glanced around, people still watched and stared, though at this point in her life, she had a hard time caring. "I wanted to protect him."

"Bullshit."

That's one of the things that Cora loved about being friends with Josephine. Josephine wasn't afraid to call her out. "If you told him you loved him, he might have chosen to stay."

"But what if he chose not to?"

"Oh, honey," Josephine's face softened. Then the announcer called Josephine's number.

Josephine said, as she gave Comet a soft kick, "The Cora I know isn't usually a coward."

Josephine kicked Comet into a trot and then sent him into a gallop as they tore down the alley for the arena, leaving Cora to stew in Josephine's parting words.

Coward.

An ugly word. A true word. Had she let him go, afraid of how badly she'd hurt if he knew she loved him, and he still didn't want to stay? She couldn't imagine the pain in her chest hurting any less than it did right now. If she were going to lose Ian, she didn't want to regret losing him because she'd feared telling him the truth.

Comet and Josephine came back from their run, to a round

of applause and shouts from the crowd. They trotted back over to her.

"That's you," Josephine said. "They called your number."

Cora glanced at her watch. There was still an hour before Ian had to board his plane.

"*Cora.*" Josephine pointed at the arena. "They called your number again. You gotta go."

You gotta go.

Cora swung down, tossing Josephine her reins. "Keys. I need your keys."

Smiling, Josephine dug her keys from her pocket. "Where you going?" As if she didn't already know.

"To tell Ian I love him."

Ian sat in the bar near his departure gate nursing a whiskey and watching the rodeo finals on television, waiting for one last chance to see Cora and Panache dash into the arena and do what they do best.

All his life, he'd never realized he had a masochistic side.

When he'd pictured this moment in his head, where he'd start his adventurous life of photojournalism by seeing the world, he hadn't expected to not want to go. Now, not only did he not want to go, but he dreaded going.

The fact that the assignment could be dangerous didn't even factor in. It all boiled down to one word. Or rather, one person...Cora.

He took another sip of whiskey. Four more riders until Cora came on. The definition of insanity had a picture of him at the bar trying to sneak one last look at the woman he loved.

Get up. Get up now. Leave. Watching her ride won't make getting on that plane and on with your life any easier.

He tossed back the last of his whiskey, grimacing as it burned a trail down the back of his esophagus. Slapping cash on the bar, he turned to leave as Josephine and Comet ran into the arena heading for the first barrel, coming in too hot and tight, brushing against the first barrel.

Ian turned and started walking out, not waiting to see if the barrel fell. See? He could do this. Cora got what she'd wanted. A fling. A distraction. Ian had been the novelty. Not the norm.

Going in, he'd known that Cora had no intention of settling down anytime soon, and when she did, it wouldn't be with a vagabond photographer, it would be with a cowboy who lived in her world.

He glanced down at his cowboy boots, that somehow felt more natural now than loafers, work boots, or tennis shoes. As much as the rodeo scene had started to feel like home, he had to remember the reality—he'd only been a city slicker on a hall pass in a cowboy town.

On the television, the announcer called out Cora's name. Ian stopped before stepping out into the terminal. *Keep walking, idiot.* Idiot that he was, Ian didn't walk, but he didn't turn around either. He waited for the familiar cheers from the crowd, the hoots and hollers and foot stomping.

Nothing came. The announcer called her name and number again.

He turned, and on mutinous feet, Ian somehow ended up back at the bar, staring up at the television, the camera focused on the alley.

No Cora. No Panache. *What the hell?*

The announcer switched to the next competitor, and the race went on with little additional comment. Missing your run wasn't unheard of. It happened occasionally for whatever reason —rider distraction, horse lameness, or any other number of reasons.

However, this was the final run. Cora wouldn't miss a chance at a check without a good reason. Had something happened to Cora? The hairs pricked on his neck and he tried to rub the feeling away. Hines had been captured and jailed and with no one willing to pay his bail, not likely to get out any time soon. Still, that heightened sense of awareness they'd all lived under until Hines had been caught left a residual unease.

On the way to the gate, he passed a bank of pay phones, then u-turned back, shaking a handful of coins from his pocket. He got the number for the rodeo office from the operator and deposited his money.

The phone rang and rang. Ian leaned back against the wall and stared out at the snow falling through the beam of the airport's exterior lights. If his flight didn't leave soon, he might not make it out of there that night and he'd miss his military connection in the morning.

After about the twentieth ring, he hung up. He tried twice more before the airlines started boarding his flight. He checked his watch. With a few minutes to spare before the doors closed he tried one last time, the ringing, unanswered phone almost mocking him.

The attendant at the counter waved at him, and called out, "Last call, Mr. Murphy."

"Coming." Ian hung up the phone.

For one crazy moment, he considered catching a cab back to the rodeo grounds, but the snow had started falling faster, big, thick, fluffy flakes. He'd be lucky to find anyone willing to drive him in that mess.

She managed before you. She'll manage without you. Her rodeo family will keep her safe.

Maybe.

Walking to the gate, he gave himself permission to call the

rodeo office again when he landed, to check up on her. The decision made him feel marginally better.

He handed the lady his ticket and she tore off his stub and handed it back to him.

As he walked down the gangway, he thought he heard Cora call out his name. He paused, then continued. That's how much she'd messed up his mind. He thought back to earlier that day, when he'd had her beneath him.

"I...I—"

Ian had broken the kiss, and she hadn't been able to meet his eyes, knowing how she felt. She didn't want a relationship. He got that. Accepted that on some level. He just hadn't wanted it pounded into his head the last few hours they had together. He'd wanted to let them both off the hook when he'd said, "I know. You don't have to say it."

He glanced behind him, and watched as the ticket agent closed the door, the latch clicking, a hard, hollow sound.

"Sir, I need you to find your seat," the stewardess standing just inside the plane said.

Ian trudged down the aisle, finding his seat. He settled in and buckled up. As the snow continued to fall, and his battered and bruised heart continued to beat in his chest, he wondered if agreeing to have sex with Cora had been the biggest mistake of his life.

Sex with someone you barely knew always carried a risk.

Pregnancy. Disease. He'd done his best to protect himself.

Too bad a prophylactic didn't protect against a broken heart.

"Come on, come on, come on," Cora yelled at the ribbon of traffic slowed by the falling snow. As rare as snow was in that part of Texas, it didn't take more than a couple of flakes to shut the whole state down. "Get out of the way."

With only one more mile until the airport exit, the snow storm continued to strengthen. She pounded her fist on the steering wheel and honked. Neither would make the cars in front of her move any faster, she knew that, but at least it felt like she was doing something.

She just needed a minute with Ian, so she pressed on, knowing the likelihood of road and airport closure increased by the minute. In fact, airport closure was something she hoped for. Maybe then her delay would give her the time she needed to tell Ian she loved him.

And the time to tell him she'd wait for him if he wanted her too.

After more yelling, fist pounding, and unfounded honking, she pulled into a parking spot and made a dash for the terminal, her boots slipping and sliding in the snow. The wind cut through her thin western shirt, and her spurs *tink*, *tinked* as she ran.

For the second time in a week, she felt like she was on the run of her life, only this time she was running toward something good, not away from something bad.

Quickly scanning the departure information board, she ran to Ian's gate, catching sight of him as he walked through the open door to the gangway. She shoved off on her right foot, trying for more speed, but the wet, slick soles of her boots slipped on the linoleum and she fell head first.

"Ian!" She called out as her body slid to a stop.

Hands grabbed her and helped her to her feet. "You okay, ma'am?" the young man asked.

"I'm fine. Thank you."

Not wasting any time, she ran toward the gate. "No, no, no," she said as the lady started closing the door to the gangway. "Wait. Please."

The door latched closed and the lady turned to her.

"Please," Cora said, "I just need one second. If I could—"

"Ma'am. You're too late. I'm sorry."

Cora's lungs bellowed as she tried to suck in air. She really needed to do what Ian did and take up running. "You're sorry."

The lady gave her a funny look, glancing to a coworker as if to say, 'you going to back me up when this lady gets crazy?'

But Cora didn't feel crazy. Just defeated.

And as the television news reporter came on and announced freeway closures, *stranded.*

––––––––

OVER THREE MONTHS LATER, IAN TRIED NOT TO FEEL DEJECTED and rejected, but after not hearing a word from Cora, and then nothing from his aunt who'd offered to call names on the list of potential fathers, it seemed like he lived his life—between skirmishes and fire fights the platoon they were embedded with got into—in mail limbo.

"No mail," Ian said as he flopped down on a cot in a tent he shared with mentor, idol, famed photographer, and now a man he could call a begrudging friend, Edward Lark.

Ed glanced up from his typewriter and grunted. The man had proved more eloquent as a photojournalist than he had as a bunk mate.

Inside the tent, outside a village the Viet Cong had mowed through, temperatures remained hot and steamy. Hot and steamy seemed the norm except when it rained. Then everything was *wet,* hot, and steamy. At least in the tent, the mosquitoes had a harder time devouring him.

He'd come to accept the permanent layer of dirt and sweat that never left his body even after a rare shower. If he stayed until the US pulled out of the country, which they'd heard rumors of for a while, his nose would probably be immune to the stench of open hole latrines, unwashed bodies, and death.

"Forget that girl back home. Plenty of locals who'd be happy to jump on your star-spangled, red, white, and blue dick—"

Ian nailed Ed with his pillow. Ed let it bounce off and kept on typing.

"Cora. Her name is Cora."

Ed grunted again. The man knew Cora's name. Refused to use it for some damn reason.

"I've given up on hearing from her if that makes you happy. I'm expecting a letter from my aunt." Ian heard the petulance in his voice, but damn if he gave two shakes of a rat's ass.

The typewriter dinged when Ed hit the return and then yanked the paper out. Ian lay with his arm over his eyes breathing in air thicker than pea soup. Here he'd thought the humidity in Texas had been bad.

Off to his right, Ian heard the tinkling of tin cups and the sound of a cork being pulled from a bottle.

Ed booted one of the legs of Ian's cot hard enough to make Ian sit up. "Here, take it," the man said.

Viet Cong hooch. Ed drank it like water. For Ian it burned more going out than it did going in. Ian took the cup. He'd pay for it later, but with the mood that had been hanging around him like a moldy feed bag, he wouldn't turn free alcohol down.

Ed sat on his cot, forgoing the cup and drinking straight from the bottle. "What's with the aunt?"

Ian eyed him over his cup, still trying to drum up the courage to take a sip. He debated telling Ed about his quest to find his father. The old coot was temperamental, a bit of an asshole, but he also listened. Though any and all advice, Ian took with a grain of salt and a long swallow of hooch.

Ian told him everything. His mother's affair. Him learning the man who'd raised him wasn't his father. The list of names

Cora had found for Ian. His aunt's efforts calling through the list to see if she could find Ian's father.

"So little Ian Murphy's looking for daddy." Make that a full-fledged asshole. "Ain't that sweet."

Ian sucked down the last of the alcohol. Didn't taste so bad after all your internal organs had gone numb. "Fuck you. I don't expect you to understand."

"Boo hoo."

"You can be a real dick sometimes."

Ed held up his hands. "Look, kid. What do you expect to get out of this?"

"I don't know. Maybe to feel connected to something. To someone."

The bottle made a popping sound when Ed pulled his lips free and swallowed. "The past is the past. Best to leave it there."

Knowing better, Ian took a chance and said, "You must have known some of the guys from your tenure at the *Times*. Anyone of them leave kids behind when they moved on? Maybe you had a drink with him and my mom at a bar or party or—"

With a heavy sigh, Ed held out a hand and made a give-it-here motion. "You got a picture of your mother?"

Ian shrugged. He had nothing to lose. Digging through his duffel, he pulled out an envelope and dumped the contents out on his cot. Along with his official press papers, he kept a few personal items. A picture of his step-father and brothers—more because it felt wrong not to bring one with him than the fact he wanted to be reminded of them— and the one of Cora kissing him on the beach. It almost seemed masochistic to keep it now, but he couldn't bring himself to toss it away.

Under a copy of the winter season rodeo schedule that he'd kept, he found the time-worn photograph of his mother holding him as an infant. His eyes flitted back to the schedule. The rodeo finals were in Houston in a little over a week. He knew where

Cora would be until then. After that, he had no idea where or when he'd be able to find her again.

He handed the photo of his mother to Ed, who had to wipe his hands dry on his pants before touching it. Ed stared at the photograph, then squinted and rubbed the sweat out of his eyes. Then threw his head back and laughed.

Ian snatched the picture out of Ed's hand and started stuffing his possessions back into the over-sized envelope. "What the hell is wrong with you, man?"

"Ol' Colleen," Ed said, wiping a tear from his eyes from laughing so hard. Ian stiffened. "That lady was one hell of a lay."

Ian raised his chin, his hands fisting at his sides. "You're telling me—"

"Boy, don't get your panties in a twist over something that happened twenty odd years ago." The alcohol must be getting into Ed's system because his sentences had topped five words.

"Twenty-five."

Ed shrugged. "So how is Colleen?"

Ian threw Ed a cutting stare that flew over the man's head. "Dead."

"Ah." The alcohol haze lifted a little, and Ed's focus cleared. "Yeah, so you've said."

"You're him."

"Apparently."

Tilting his head, Ian took in this man who'd slept with his mother, trying to see something of himself in the man sitting across from him. Maybe in the color of his eyes or his smile. But Ian didn't have that cruel curve, that Ed's smile sometimes took. Ian waited for some sort of primal recognition, some connection, but he felt...nothing.

Ed didn't seem phased or moved by the news. Had his mother meant anything to Ed? Or had she only been 'a hell of a lay?' "Did you know about me?"

Ed shook his head. "If it makes you feel any better, I wouldn't have stuck around anyway."

"How many half-brothers or sisters do I have out there?"

Ed shrugged again, his body language as effusive as his spoken language. "Dunno."

Reaching across, Ed poured the last of the hooch into Ian's cup. "Drink up, son."

"Don't ever call me that." Ian stood, needing to walk or run, or *something*. Anything, anywhere as long as Ed wasn't there.

He headed toward the tent flap when Ed said, "Hey, kid."

Stopping, Ian turned, and Ed threw Ian's helmet at him. "Keep your head down."

———

CORA HELD PANACHE'S REINS AS SHE LED HIM BENEATH THE stands of the Houston Astrodome, home of the Houston Livestock Show and Rodeo. Tonight was the last night. The final round. A lot of money riding on the outcome of the race that night. Enough to get Cora through the next season if she counted her pennies.

"Hey, wait up."

Cora stopped, and Levi jogged over, his chestnut quarter horse Chunk trotting at the end of his reins.

Levi fell into step beside her and threw a companionate arm around her shoulder. "You know, we can go behind the restrooms for a good luck fuck if you think it would help you with your run tonight." Levi grinned, cheesy and wide.

Cora threw her head back and laughed, almost regretting ever telling Levi about how she'd approached Ian for sex. At least now she could laugh about it.

Olivia Marsh, the owner of No Bull, the roughstock company, who'd taken over after Hines had gotten himself arrested, cut Levi a look as she walked by. "You really are a pig, Banks."

Levi dropped his arm from Cora's shoulder and glanced behind him at the tall blond. "It was a joke," he hollered out.

Then to Cora said, "I was joking."

"I know."

"Where did that come from? I don't know what I did wrong, but she's been on my ass since Hines got arrested. It's not my fault her employee was a douchebag asshole and got exactly what he deserved."

Cora waggled her brows. "Maybe she likes you. Maybe her treating you like the scum beneath her boot is like the little boys who used to dip little girls' pig tails into the ink wells at school."

"Ah...no. Olivia's smart, beautiful, and just as soon see me drawn and quartered than give me the time of day."

"Like you said, smart woman."

Levi tugged her into him and gave her a smacking kiss on the top of her head. "Thanks, Hayes. I don't know what my ego would do without you."

Overhead, the announcer came over the PA giving the order of the first five barrel racers after the upcoming arena drag. "Don't you have to be somewhere?" Cora asked.

"I've got time to watch your run."

"You don't have—"

"I like being there for you."

Cora gave him a warning look. "Says the man who just broke up with his girlfriend."

"As a friend only. Lord knows I can't compete with Ian's ghost."

At the mention of Ian's name her chest constricted, and she had to suck air in through her mouth to get enough oxygen. She'd called Josephine's father at his ranch religiously once a week waiting on a return letter from Ian.

Called and waited for nothing.

Despite all the letters she'd sent him, telling him how much she loved him. How she'd wait for him. But after a few months of radio static, even Josephine had a hard time coming up with believable excuses as to why Ian hadn't written back.

It was way past time for Cora to move on. She'd worked and trained hard and proved to herself these past few months that she didn't need a man to win. But it sure as hell would have been nice to have one by her side to celebrate when she did.

Levi brushed a thumb under her eye, where the bags and bruising from her lack of sleep were receding. "You've been sleeping better it seems."

She nodded. "I have."

"You moved on?"

"Yeah," she said, but with the way her voice cracked, the lie didn't fly.

The announcer called the first racer, and Levi and Chunk backed up a couple steps, so Cora could swing up into the saddle.

"Cora?" Levi said as he started to lead Chunk away.

"Yeah?"

"Kick some ass out there."

Cora shoved her hat down farther on her head and smiled down at Levi. "I plan on it."

A few minutes later, the announcer called out Cora's name and number and she trotted into the alley.

"Go, Cora!" Josephine yelled and clapped from behind the alley fence.

As much as Cora wished Ian were there, she knew that if she ran clean, she had as good of a chance of winning as anybody. It had taken Ian leaving and Cora continuing to win for her to know that she had what it took to make it big in barrel racing. To put up fast runs. To show the world what she and Panache were made of.

Ian's dick hadn't been magic, it hadn't made her win, but Ian's love and patience and faith in her and her abilities continued to fuel her. Knowing that one person in the world believed in her with all his heart...*that* was magic.

Tonight, she planned on winning. Not to show him. Not to show the world. But to show herself.

"Let's go, boy," Cora said as she kicked Panache into a gallop.

They burst into the arena, the enormous crowd packing the Astrodome, deafening. She couldn't hear the thunder of Panache's hooves or the roar of his breathing, but as she headed for the first barrel, she felt all of her horse's heart.

Cheers and adrenaline fueled them, Panache rated his speed at the first barrel, digging hard and deep with his back legs skirting the barrel with inches to spare, then hurtling for the second barrel. The second and third barrels flew by in a flurry of flying dirt and dust.

Sweat broke out on Panache's neck as Cora stood in the stirrups and held her hands and reins up his neck as Panache shifted into another gear. The wind stung her eyes and she couldn't see her time as she rocketed back down the alley.

She sat deep in the saddle, gradually slowing Panache to a walk. A small cheer went up from the other riders beneath the stands and she slapped Josephine's hand as her friend trotted by for her own run.

Panache pranced sideways, still amped up from all the excitement. Cora jumped down and pulled the reins over her horse's head. Over to her left, she spotted Levi and Chunk. He pumped his fist in the air and clapped.

Then Levi's focus shifted, and his smile got wider. He bumped his chin toward something behind her. "Look."

"What?"

Panache panted in her left ear.

"Behind you," he shouted.

Cora turned, running smack into a hard chest. Hands came up to steady her. "I'm sorry, I—"

"Hello, Cora."

She knew that voice. Knew the chemical smell. Developer and fixer and dreams she didn't dare dream. Slowly she looked up, almost afraid that he wasn't really there. But he was. His hair was shorter beneath his cowboy hat. His body leaner beneath her fingers. "Ian."

Before she could say anything else, Levi walked over and shook Ian's hand and took Panache's reins. "You two go. I'll take care of Panache."

"But—"

Levi started backing away, taking the horses with him. "Don't argue."

She turned back to Ian, still not believing her eyes. "How?—Why?—"

"Hold that thought." He linked his fingers with hers and dragged her through the tunnels beneath the stadium and pushed through the exit doors, dumping them out into a parking lot with a sea of cars, trucks, and trailers.

The stadium doors closed behind them, trapping the chaos inside. The stars hung high, the temperature mild even for late February in Houston.

Ian leaned back against the building and pulled her between his legs. "Hey, there."

His hands cupped her neck, his thumb tracing over the pulse thrumming at the base of her collarbone, his eyes drinking her in.

"Hey, there yourself."

"Put your hands on my shirt and hold on tight."

"Why's that?"

"Just do it."

She did. "Now what?"

"Now I'm going to kiss you, Cora Hayes."

He ducked his head, but she pressed a finger to his lips. "What if I don't want to be kissed?"

Ian raised an amused brow, his gaze flicked from her eyes to her lips and back again. He didn't say anything, he just waited.

"Okay fine," Cora said. "You can kiss me."

That time, when Ian leaned in, she didn't stop him. She also didn't stop him when he led her to his rental car and took her to a hotel with a room overlooking the Astrodome.

"It's beautiful," she said as she stared out the window at all the lights from the city and the carnival on the far side of the dome.

Ian came up behind her, and threaded his arms around her waist, kissing the back of her neck, and breathing her in deep. "I missed your smell. Pine shavings, horse sweat, and sass."

Cora laughed, turning in his arms, her words soft, but serious when she said, "I missed you."

"I called." Ian brushed his hands up and down her back, before finally settling on the curve of her ass, holding her against him. "That night when I left. I called from the airport when you didn't ride. I thought you might be hurt or—"

She rested her forehead against his, her whispered words falling from her lips. "Oh my God."

With a finger under her chin, he tilted her head up. "What?"

"I came after you. Fighting through the traffic and the snow. I ran to the gate. I called out, but I was too late."

Ian closed his eyes and for a second there, Cora wasn't sure he was still breathing. When he opened them again, his eyes were glassy. "Why did you come?"

"I didn't want you to leave without knowing the truth. That I loved you."

"Loved?" He said, his voice tentative. "Past tense?"

Cora didn't hesitate. "No. Present tense love. I loved you then. I love you now."

"Oh, baby." Ian folded his arms around her and pulled her into his chest. Beneath her ear, his heart beat, a rapid erratic thumping matching her own. He took her hands and tugged her back with him to the bed and sat, leaning against the headboard.

He pulled her into his lap and shucked her boots. "Would you have asked me to stay?"

"I don't know," she answered with all honesty. "I wouldn't have wanted you to pass up your dream for me. But then I got selfish and sent those letters asking you to come home anyway."

"What letters?"

"The ones—" Cora glanced up at him. He wasn't pretending. "You never got my letters?"

He shook his head. "You get mine?"

"No." She ran her hand over the scruff on his jaw. "But you came anyway."

"I found my father," he said, but before she could say anything, he added, "funny story, but it can wait. But in finding him, I realized the piece of me that was missing wasn't out there in the wild world, it was back here. With you."

He put his hand over her heart and it kicked back against her chest. "I've got no money. Just a truck and camper in storage a couple hours away. But this is where I belong, if you'll still have me."

"Yes," she said, as the grin took over her face.

He pulled her in for a crushing kiss. Their teeth clashed, but neither of them cared. He took the kiss deeper, as the blood rushed to her core, and her fingers fumbled with his belt.

Breaking the kiss, he said, "I need you naked, woman."

"You think I'm easy."

"I do." When he grinned down at her that way, all she wanted to do was strip him bare and have her way with him.

She gave him a playful swat. "I promised myself if I ever saw you again I wouldn't fall straight into your bed until I told you how I really felt."

"To be fair," he said as he unbuttoned her shirt, button by button, "this isn't my bed, I'm here too, so I'm just as easy as you are, and finally, you told me how you felt, so no broken promises."

"I still think I'm too easy."

Cora unbuckled his belt, and pulled it free, her breath catching as he nibbled his way down her neck toward her breast. He unsnapped her bra and groaned as he took her nipple into his mouth. Her head fell back, and she held his head in place.

He shifted, her nipple coming free with a soft *pop*. "That's just the way I love you."

LETTER TO MY READERS

Dear Reader,

Take a moment to grab a beer and dust off the dirt, because it's about time bulldogger, Levi Banks, found a good woman.

Unfortunately, Olivia Marsh, the sexy owner of *No Bull Roughstock Supply* thinks he's a cad. And worse.

When unexpected news is dropped into his lap, is it a blessing, or a curse? All Levi knows is it will take all of him to make his new life work.

Olivia is no fool and she won't be taken in by Levi's slow, sexy smile the same way her cousin had been. She knows the truth about Levi. But when his life is upended in the middle of the spring circuit, she begins to question everything she knows about that man.

Can she risk her heart? Or is true love just a silly myth?

Now gather up your reins and dig in your spurs...*Reined In* is a hot read for a cold night.

ABOUT THE AUTHOR

Vicki Tharp makes her home on small acreage in south Texas with her husband and an embarrassing number of pets. When she isn't writing, you can usually find her on the back of her horse—avoiding anything that remotely resembles housework—smelling like fly spray and horse sweat.

Join my newsletter at: http://eepurl.com/croJgz
Join my street team and receive free Advance Reader Copies of my upcoming books at: http://eepurl.com/cWhXbD
You can find my website at: www.VickiTharp.com
I love to hear from readers. You can email me at
Author@VickiTharp.com

Or you can stalk me at:

facebook.com/VickiTharpAuthor

twitter.com/vwtharp

instagram.com/author_Vicki_Tharp

amazon.com/author/vicki_tharp

bookbub.com/authors/vicki-tharp